Rittenhouse

Rittenhouse

The Saga of an American Family

Volume 2

A Novel

J.D. Rittenhouse

Library of Congress Control Number:		2019912250
ISBN:	Hardcover	978-1-7960-5411-8
	Softcover	978-1-7960-5410-1
	eBook	978-1-7960-5409-5

Photo Credit: Mariah Shotts

Original work and research by J.D. Rittenhouse, edited by Shanna McLean
(ShannaPra@gmail.com)

Partial Revisions, additional research, and final editing by
Michelle Rittenhouse-LaSalle

Print information available on the last page.

Rev. date: 09/06/2019

To order additional copies of this book, contact:
Xlibris
1-888-795-4274
www.Xlibris.com
Orders@Xlibris.com
797621

CHAPTER 1

A tall man in his middle forties cautiously peered around the corner of a shop in the Boston Square. He stayed hidden in the darkness of the shadows, careful not to let his presence be known. Over the last twenty years he had learned to be very guarded.

He heard men shouting at each other while he was on his way home. He was curious, but not to the point of exposing himself to unknown circumstances. As he looked on, he saw several Americans scuffling with three British soldiers in front of a rope maker's shop.

He didn't know what the argument was about, but then, in early March 1770, arguments which consisted of shouting and shoving between American and British soldiers were commonplace in Boston and other cities. In late January of that year, New York members of the Sons of Liberty clashed with 40 British soldiers who were posting broadsheets. Several men were seriously injured in the fighting.

Bostonians had been protesting and rioting since the passage of the Townshend Acts. As a result, an unusually high number of British soldiers now patrolled the city.

The man in the shadows on the night of March 2nd, was Crispus Attucks, a molatto of African and American Indian descent. About twenty years earlier he had escaped from William Brown of Framingham. Brown had owned Crispus' entire family as slaves. After running away, he changed his name to Michael Johnson and secured employment as a harpooner on a whaling ship. He later became a laborer.

His cautious vigilance came not only from the fact that he was a runaway slave but also from the life he lived. As a seaman, he was constantly in danger of being impressed into the British Navy. As a laborer, he was in competition with British soldiers who often took jobs as part-time laborers during their off-duty hours and would work for less money.

After watching the foray between the British soldiers and the rope makers that Friday evening, he decided the fracas was nothing in which he wished to participate. He quietly and inconspicuously faded into the shadows.

The next night, March 3rd, another scuffle between the rope makers and British soldiers occurred. Crispus did not bother to make it to the square to observe that squabble. In retrospect, he thanked God that he had not been there. The scuffle that night left a British soldier with a fractured skull.

The next day, and even the day after, Crispus heard discussions and rumors indicating that more serious trouble was brewing for the city of Boston. Rumors that the British soldiers were going to get revenge and the townspeople were going to fight it out with the soldiers had been circulating for two days.

As daylight turned to dusk, on March 5th, Hugh White, a British private, stood guard as a group of Boston townsmen and British soldiers crossed paths near his sentry box. He had just finished talking to one of his captains. As the captain was leaving the sentry box, White heard a young man in the crowd, Edward Garrick, yell out, "That was the fellow that won't pay my master for addressing his hair." The captain ignored the young man and continued walking away. White, however, thought the captain's honor should be defended. He approached Garrick and told him that as a British officer a captain would pay his bill to Garrick's employer. Garrick, unsatisfied, began hurling insults.

White went into a rage swinging the butt of his rifle into the young man's head. Garrick slumped to the ground. Several townspeople rushed to Garrick's aid when they saw him fall. When it became clear that he had been hit in the head by White, the townspeople began taunting White and pelting him with snowballs.

White sought cover on the steps of the nearby Custom House while he loaded his musket. The townspeople continued their barrage of insults and snowballs aimed at White.

Suddenly, the peal of church bells could be heard. Thinking there was a fire, about 50 more men ran to the scene. White, fearing for his life, backed up to the locked front door of the Custom House and began yelling for help.

White's calls for help were heard and soon seven British soldiers led by Capt. Thomas Preston arrived on the scene. He ordered his men to form a semi-circle around White. As the townspeople started closing in, the soldiers began waving their bayonets in an attempt to ward off any attack.

What started out as a confrontation between a British soldier and a few Bostonians now involved eight British soldiers facing off against several hundred townspeople. Crispus, responding to the church bells, had been caught up in the surge of the mass of people and was forced to the front of the mob.

When the crowd was ordered to disperse and return to their homes by Capt. Preston, their response became angrier as they hurled insults and a barrage of snowballs. Then they began taunting the soldiers by daring them to shoot. Capt. Preston indicated that he had no intention of firing into the crowd.

Without warning, a wooden club came hurtling out of the mass of humanity, striking a private by the name of Hugh Montgomery, knocking him to the ground. Montgomery rose to his feet and raised his weapon. As he discharged his musket into the air, he yelled "Damn you! Fire!"

One of the local rope makers, Richard Palms, struck Montgomery with a stick. Then he gave Capt. Preston a whack on the arm. Confusion reigned. Quickly the British soldiers let loose a round of musket fire. Crispus Attucks, who this night had thrown caution to the wind and joined the crowd, crumpled to the ground. Two musket balls hit him in the chest, killing him instantly. By the time the melee was over, five Bostonians lay dead in the street. Six more had been wounded.

Crispus' body was carried to Faneuil Hall. It lay in state until Thursday, March 8, when Crispus and the other victims were buried together. All were hailed as martyrs. Later Crispus would come to be known as the first victim of the Revolution.

A few days later Preston and his men were taken into custody as a result of the protests of the townspeople over the killings. Mobs gathered, demanding punishment for the soldiers. The protesters wanted swift justice and didn't care if that constituted a fair trial or not.

John Adams, Samuel Adams' cousin, believed in the rebels' cause, but also believed the soldiers should get a fair trial. Risking his reputation, and possibly his life, he teamed with attorney, Joshua Quincey, to represent Capt. Preston and his men. All were cleared of any wrong-doing except for Montgomery and a private named Matthew Kilroy who were convicted for their parts in setting off the shootings. Both men were sentenced to be branded with an "M," for murderer, on their thumb with a hot iron.

The incident became known as the "Boston Massacre". It also became a rallying point for the patriots. As a result of the "Massacre," the colonies hovered on the periphery of war for several days. Pamphlets and essays were soon circulating among the colonies about the incident. Some were sympathetic to the Americans, while others took the side of the British soldiers.

For several weeks the Boston shootings were frequently discussed by David Rittenhouse and his brother-in-law, Thomas Barton. Barton, the consummate loyalist, saw the incident as an unfortunate conflict between Bostonian ruffians who had set out to cause trouble and British soldiers who were simply doing their duty.

David, on the other hand, believed the English government had become oppressive and the intolerant of the rights of the colonists. He saw the melee as an accumulation of frustration over the oppressive laws the crown had been imposing on Americans.

While neither one of them could understand the others point of view or be persuaded by arguments of the other, the two men remained steadfast and loyal to one another. They refused to let whatever differences they had interfere with either their personal or familial relationships.

One thing they did agree upon was the devastating effect the Townshend Acts were having on the colonies. They were at odds over the right of Parliament to impose taxes on the colonies even though America was not represented in Parliament. David, as did a majority of Americans, agreed with the concept that the colonies should not be taxed without representation in Parliament. Barton believed the English had the right to tax the colonies, but he also believed that that right was being abused and that the revenue acts should be revised to be more tolerant.

They did not realize it at the time but on the same day the Boston massacre occurred, Lord Frederick North, the new Prime Minister of England, introduced legislation in Parliament to repeal all the tea duty portion of the act. Both men congratulated each other when they learned North's repeal was given the Royal sign of approval on April 16th.

David, while well aware of the continuing unrest in the colonies, had more immediate concerns. He was close to putting the finishing touches on his first orrery. In addition, his wife, Eleanor, was again pregnant. She expected delivery around late winter.

Barton, Smith and others had been lobbying David to move to Philadelphia where he could enjoy greater exposure. The more he delayed the greater the pressure became from those urging him to make the move.

Eleanor had noticed the strain that David had been under for several weeks. Even with her, David was slow to share his feelings. Usually she would show restraint when it came to quizzing her husband about things that were bothering him. She knew how private he was about such things. Now however, David was showing more stress than usual.

"I know how private you are about things that are troubling you, but I have never seen you so stressed before. Please tell me what has you so troubled," she asked him one evening in October as they sat down to eat supper.

David looked at her for a moment, contemplating her question. Usually he did not involve her in his work or his daily life. While she was an intelligent woman, he knew the things he worked on and the things he thought about would either not interest her or, like most people, would be beyond her comprehension. But this was different. This time it involved her and he knew he did not have the right to make a decision without discussing it with her.

"Thomas and Dr. Smith, and other people in the Society, and in the legislature, have been urging me for some time to move to Philadelphia. While they know we are perfectly comfortable here in Norriton, they seem to believe it would be beneficial for my work if we moved to the city." He waited for her response.

"Why does that have you troubled?" she asked as she sat down at the table. "If you do not want to go, tell them so. If you want to go, we will move. It seems fairly straightforward to me."

"I wish it were that simple. Everyone also seems to be pushing me to complete my work on the orreries as soon as possible. If we move I would have to be put them on hold while I built another workshop."

David got up from the table and walked to the kitchen window. He stood there gazing out the window for a couple of minutes. Finally he turned to Eleanor with a look in his eyes she had never seen. She waited for him to speak.

"I am very concerned over the fact the move may have an adverse effect on your condition."

She assured him that if he decided to move to Philadelphia, the move would in no way imperil her, the new baby, or the girls, who now were two and four years of age. While that eased his mind a little, deep down he was still concerned, but he decided to keep his concerns to himself.

Finally in late 1770, David agreed to move himself, Eleanor, and their two baby daughters to Philadelphia. By that time David himself had come to the realization that, even though his work was applauded and recognized in wider and wider circles, he could not achieve his full promise by remaining in Norriton.

David's younger brother, Benjamin, who still lived on their father's farm in Worchester Township, also been making a name for himself as well. In addition to gaining notoriety as a clockmaker and a maker of surveyor's instruments, both of which he learned from his older brother. Benjamin had also become a well-known gun smith.

Benjamin traveled from the Worchester to Philadelphia to help David construct a new workshop. It was then he informed David that a year earlier he had commenced courting Elizabeth Bull, the daughter of John and Mary Bull. Their wedding, he told David, was set for December 26.

David was familiar with John Bull's reputation. Bull had served under a commission from Queen Anne as a captain and the Third Battalion, Pennsylvania Regiment at Fort Allen in Carbon County. He had also accompanied Brig. Gen. John Forbes and Col. George Washington in an expedition to capture Fort Duquesne from the French in 1754.

The expedition did not reach Fort Duquesne until 1758, and then, only after Bull helped in the negotiations of the Treaty of Easton which undercut the alliance between the Native Americans of the region and the French. This ultimately allowed the British to seize control of Fort Duquesne. He later retired to the farm his father had left him in the Limerick Township.

Shortly after the move David's life in Philadelphia, socially at least, began to take hold. At the first meeting of the Philosophical Society in January, he was elected secretary and at the beginning of February he delivered what was described as a fascinating paper on the mesmerizing ability of snakes.

David's relocation to Philadelphia, however, did not come without a price. As the days passed, it became evident to David that his beloved Eleanor was having a difficult time with her pregnancy.

"I wish I had more time to spend with you," he told her one evening while they were preparing for bed. "But I have so much pressure on me to complete the orrery for Dr. Witherspoon. It appears everyone in the world is waiting for it to be completed."

"It's all right, I know how important your work is to you," she said, gently patting his hand. "According to Thomas, the orrery is important to the whole of America, and you must complete it as quickly as possible."

Barton was right. The whole of America, especially those involved in the philosophies, were anxiously anticipating the completion of David's machine for the glory of the country.

At one point, the Pennsylvania Journal and Weekly Advertiser printed an article praising the orrery as "an American production and much more complete than anything of the–kind ever in Europe. It must give great pleasure to every lover of his country to see her rising to fame in the sublime science as well as every improvement in the arts."

In April, a prominent Philadelphia newspaper reported "Dr. Weatherspoon, accompanied by some gentlemen, went on Saturday to see and converse with the ingenious artist, and being convinced of the superior advantages that must rise from this new invented orrery. And its desire is to encourage so truly great a genius, purchased it for the use of the College of New Jersey."

Dr. William Smith, Provost of the College of Philadelphia, had other ideas. He thought the first orrery should go to the college. After all Smith was instrumental in nurturing David's reputation to the point of intercontinental notoriety. In addition, the college of Philadelphia was the first to convey an honorary degree upon David. This created a dilemma for David who had agreed to sell the first orrery to Dr. Weatherspoon.

To resolve the dilemma, Weatherspoon agreed to provide the orrery for display in Philadelphia when it was completed, giving David and Dr. Smith the opportunity to hold lectures on the orrery. The lectures were meant as a way of raising money which would allow the College of Philadelphia to purchase its own orrery.

The mechanisms of the orrery were placed in a Chippendale case exquisitely handcrafted by Parnell Gibbs and John Folwell, two of Philadelphia's finest joiners. David had once described the orrery in a letter to Barton. He wrote that the machine would have three faces, the largest of which would be four feet square which would be made of sheet brass and exquisitely ornate.

In the center of the face would be a gilded brass ball representing the sun. Other balls, made of brass or ivory, represented planets. The balls would move elliptically around the ball representing the sun. The motion of the stars and planets would at times speed up or slow down according to their natural motions.

The real beauty of the machine, however, came not from its ornate design, but from the fact that it was so accurate that it could foretell the position of the planets and stars for a period of 5000 years in advance or 5000 years in the past. It was a machine that drew applause and amazement on both sides of the Atlantic.

At the beginning of February, David's friend, Israel Jacobs, who was a member of the Pennsylvania Assembly, asked David if he could write a description of the orrery so he could bring David's invention to the attention of the lawmakers. David obliged Jacobs, though he hated the distraction it caused him. Eleanor was about to go into labor and David wanted to spend as much time as possible beside her bed.

David's concerns about Eleanor's condition were not misplaced. On February 21, 1771, she went into labor. It was difficult for David to watch his beloved wife writhe with pain. Finally after several hours she delivered a son. David watched as the child was extracted from the womb.

David's first emotion was to be glad that the ordeal was over. However, whatever ecstasy David may have felt soon turned to grief for him and Eleanor.

The baby was still born. In addition, it was clear to everyone attending to her that Eleanor was having complications after the delivery. She was in agony, perspiration covering her body like a blanket. She was continuously passing in and out of consciousness for the next two days.

Then she, like her baby boy, was gone!

David had never felt so betrayed by life. "How irksome does everything seem," he told Barton shortly after the funerals. "Nothing interesting, nothing entertaining accept my two little girls; and yet my reflecting on their loss sinks me the deeper in affliction."

Barton attempted to be consoling. He genuinely had deep concerned about David's despair, but he little understood the emotions welling up in David. Dr. William Smith was even slower to realize the agony David was going through and often made lighthearted remarks about getting David through his agony as quickly as possible. David stumbled through the days without truly comprehending what was going on around him.

Even the fact that the first volume of the American Philosophical Society *Transactions* was published and celebrated him and his orrery and his observations of the transit of Venus could not bring David out of his doldrums.

His only salvation came from work. He was heavily involved in giving lectures on his orrery and other philosophical topics. The more he worked the more accolades and remunerations he received. But his depression continued.

"It would seem to me, if I were in your position of receiving great applause and financial rewards that you receive, the grayness about my life would be lifted," Barton told David one day as they were discussing David's melancholy.

"This would have been very agreeable to me, if my poor Eleanor had lived; but now, neither money nor reputation has any charms, though I must still think them valuable as absolutely necessary in this unhappy life. The only thing that gives me pleasure are my two little girls," David confided to his brother-in-law.

Early in April David delivered the promised orrery to Dr. Weatherspoon. He then commenced work on two additional orreries, one for the college of Philadelphia, and the other for the city of Philadelphia.

He was slowly regaining interest in the Philosophical Society. However, he could not belie the fact that he was still grieving for his Eleanor. He was still haunted by the idea that the move to Philadelphia may have contributed to the miscarriage of the baby and death of his wife. Even though he was resuming his active life he found little joy or pleasure and anything.

Barton continually complained of David's failure to write. Finally, David responded to the complaints. "That you may not be disappointed, I would have you to expect nothing of me in the future. I no longer feel any inducement to exert myself. Everything in life, even life itself, is insipid."

On March 8, 1772 the Pennsylvania Assembly passed a resolution awarding David £ 300, "as a testimony of the high sense which this House entertains of his Mathematical Genius and Mechanical Abilities and constructing the said Orrery."

David had become friends with Charles Willson Peale who was, among other things, interested in sciences. His greatest achievements, however, was with the paintbrush and easel. His paintings of George Washington, John Hancock, and Benjamin Franklin had gained him much notoriety.

Peale, like most educated people in the colonies, admired David's work and forthrightness. In the early part of 1772, he convinced David to let him paint his portrait. Peale was forthcoming with David, telling him he was going to produce engravings of the portrait to be sold to an adoring public.

This was a time when American accomplishments were still in the shadow of England and Europe. Any accomplishments, whether in the sciences or arts, were gaged against English and European accomplishments in those fields. Any accolades from across the sea had special import for the colonies.

In April, Benjamin Franklin who at that time was representing the colonies in London, sent a box of books to the Philosophical Society along with a letter from the Rev. William Ludlam. Ludlam was a prominent English educator and a fellow of St. John's College, Cambridge.

The letter came with specific instructions that it be directed to David Rittenhouse. The letter heaped praise on the society's *Transactions* and specifically called out David's work.

Ludlam wrote, *"There is not another Society in the world that can boast of a member such as Mr. Rittenhouse: theorist enough to encounter the problems of determining (from a few Observations) the Orbit of a Comet; and also mechanic enough to make, with his own hands, an Equal-Altitude Instrument, a Transit-Telescope, and the Timepiece. I wish I was near enough to see his mechanical apparatus."*

Princeton College and Dr. Weatherspoon were so proud of the fact that they had David's first orrery that they used it in advertising to attract new students. The college was so pleased that in September it bestowed an honorary degree of Master of Arts on David.

In September David was approached by James Humphrey, the publisher of the *Universal Almanac*. He asked David if he would be interested in supplying astronomical calculations for his publication. "Publications such as mine, if relying on calculations and data prepared by as great a mathematician as yourself, will give them stamp of the validity. As you know good Sir, all data now supplied to almanacs are based on calculations derived at Boston. Calculations derived in Philadelphia, especially by so eminent a mathematician as yourself would be highly prized."

David agreed to provide the publisher with the risings and settings of the sun, the length of the days, and some data on the movement of planets and the moon. Humphrey knew that having David's name associated with the almanac was more important than the actual data that David produced.

In advertising for his almanac Humphrey stated: *"The calculations of this Almanac may be depended upon, as performed with the greatest exactness and truth, being the performance of that ingenious master of mathematics Mr. David Rittenhouse, of this City."*

It was not long before David was supplying other almanac publisher's data for their publications. At least a dozen publishers proudly advertised that David had provided the calculations for their almanacs. Within eight years David became so overwhelmed with the demands for his calculations for almanacs that he had to decline supplying them.

It was about this time that David became involved in a land claim dispute between Pennsylvania and Virginia. The dispute involved settlers who had their families moved into an area claimed by both states. Some of the families had land patents from one of the two states and other families had no written claim.

David and Dr. William Smith thought they had a solution to the problem. They presented their plan for an astronomical survey to Surveyor General John Lukens.

The plan involved quietly determining whether Fort Pitt was in the Pennsylvania or Virginia. The information could then be used to help Gov. Penn in his negotiations with the governor of Virginia.

The survey established that Fort Pitt was within Pennsylvania borders. The survey, which was done without notice or knowledge of Virginia remained a Pennsylvania secret until January, 1774 when any dispute between the states was eclipsed by the Revolutionary War.

David often spent evenings in the parlor of his long-standing friends, the Jacobs brothers, John and Israel Jacobs, in friendly discussions concerning current events and their philosophies concerning them.

Hannah Jacobs, their sister was usually present during these discussions. As the loss of Eleanor became more distant David grew fonder of Hannah who was three years David's junior. She, as had been Eleanor, was a member of the Society of Friends.

David knew Hannah to be very bright and well-informed. She was also a very patient and efficient person which had all the more attraction for David. In September David asked for her hand in marriage. She agreed. They were married in a quiet ceremony on December 31, 1772, in her brother's parlor.

CHAPTER 2

David's two little girls, Elizabeth and Ester, who had known Hannah all of their lives, had little problem accepting her as their mother. As the family settled into their new lives, David found that he was at peace with himself for the first time since Eleanor had passed away. In February, Hannah informed David that she was pregnant. She said she thought her delivery would be late October or early November.

By March, the realization of a potential war with Britain was becoming clearer, not only to David, but to the rest of the colonists as well.

Later that month, David received a letter from his good friend, Thomas Jefferson, informing him that the Virginia House of Burgesses had appointed Jefferson, Patrick Henry, Richard Henry Lee and nine others to a committee of correspondence. The committee, according to Jefferson, was formed to communicate with other colonies regarding the growing complaints against the British.

In the letter, Jefferson encouraged David to involve himself in Pennsylvania politics and to encourage Pennsylvania to follow Virginia's lead.

"I know, my dear friend, Rittenhouse, that you are a peaceful man of science, but I also know that more and more our country will be tested by the insufferable greed of Parliament. At some point, it is going to be the duty of all patriotic Americans, of

which I know you are to be counted, to resist the continued
oppression of the English government."

Jefferson's admonishment to David was still fresh in his mind when word arrived that King George had signed a new law on May 10. This law was called the Tea Act and would have repercussions, not only in America and England, but around the world.

David, heeding his friend's advice, became more active in the radical Philadelphia Mechanics Association. Most members of the Association were avid supporters of the independence movement, and while David was sympathetic to the movement, he had yet to become involved in its politics. That was about to change.

By June, several other states, upon hearing the details of the Tea Act and following Virginia's lead, formed committees of correspondence of their own. The Act imposed 3 pence per pound tax on tea imported to America, which was lower than the tax imposed by the Townshend Acts. Many in England thought this would please the colonists. However, the colonists viewed it as more oppression.

Tea could be brought into America only on East India Company ships. Before this, American ships were unable to import tea. Also, agents appointed by the East India Company, many of whom were friends or relatives of the Royally appointed colonial governors, could only sell the tea.

It soon became clear that the Tea Act was going to have a major impact on shipowners and merchants. The usually reticent shop owners became aligned with such radicals as Samuel Adams in voicing their concerns about, and in opposition to the Act.

In July, the Philosophical Society imported an electric eel to study. Others scientists had been studying the eel's shock to determine whether it was electrical or if there was another explanation for it.

David was appointed to a committee to study the eels. After several experiments, it was concluded by the committee that since the eel's shock could not pass through "dry wood, glass, or any other substance" that the eel did, in fact, produce electricity.

In late September, word reached the colonies that ships laden with over 500,000 pounds of tea were headed from England to America. On October 10, Ben Franklin, owner, and publisher of the *Pennsylvania Gazette,* published a searing editorial he called "a statement of resolutions opposing the Tea Act," calling the Act unfair, and that it amounted to the imposition of an "arbitrary government and slavery" upon American citizens.

The resolutions urged opposition to the Act by all, stating that anyone who transported, sold or consumed the taxed tea would be considered "an enemy to his country." The statement would become known as the "Philadelphia Resolutions."

Soon after Franklin published the statement, Hannah went into labor. Throughout the pregnancy, David, mindful that a difficult delivery caused the death of Eleanor, constantly lived with the fear of history repeating itself. It was hard to keep this thought out of his mind.

David's black servant, Annie, was called to act as a midwife when Hannah's labor became more intense. Upon her arrival, David was exiled to another room where he waited with Annie's husband, Julius, anxiously pacing back and forth with heavy steps. At one point, David's pacing became so loud that Annie had to ask him to pace with lighter steps.

Suddenly, after two days of listening to Hannah moan with intense labor, David heard nothing! There were no shrieks of pain coming from the bedroom, but neither was there the cry of a newborn baby. Petrified, David arose from the chair he had been sleeping in and walked toward the bedroom. Just as he was about to enter, Annie emerged.

"Miss Hannah is sleeping comfortably now, but the baby died while still in the womb." He heard Annie's voice echo wall-to-wall. Suddenly he realized what she was saying, 'Hannah was fine, but the baby was stillborn.'

"Was the baby a boy or a girl, Annie?" he asked, too saddened and shocked by the news of the baby's death, he didn't know what to say at that moment.

"It was a boy, Mister David," he heard Annie say, as she finished cleaning up. David slowly walked to the parlor where he slumped into a chair. He hadn't realized until now how much he had wanted a male heir.

He dropped his head to his hands and covering his eyes he allowed himself a deep sigh and a slight tear. Then suddenly, he realized that the main priority was not him, it was Hannah. Walking back into the bedroom, Annie reassured him that Hannah would be fine.

Later that month, members of the Philadelphia Son of Liberty formed committees that forced the East India Company tea agents in Philadelphia to resign. Most of the agents resigned as the results of threats and intimidation. As far as the Patriots were concerned, their methods were effective. As ships arrived in Philadelphia, they were turned away without paying any tax on their tea.

In Boston, however, the Sons of Liberty, following the lead of Philadelphians, were unsuccessful in their attempts to make the tea agents resign. As a result, Boston Harbor was the site of three ships full of tea.

On November 29, a mass meeting led by Samuel Adams, John Hancock, and other radicals, attempted to determine the fate of the three tea ships. That meeting had an inconclusive ending.

Resuming the meeting on November 30, it decided the radicals would attempt to send the "Dartmouth" back to England, without paying the tax. Governor Thomas Hutchison ignored their warnings.

On December 16, Samuel Adams told a gathering of approximately 8,000 Bostonians about the governor's refusal to let the ships sail out of the harbor unless the tax on the tea they carried was paid. The crowd, whipped into a frenzy by Adams, began shouting anti-British slogans and making threats against Hutchison.

With the crowd still milling around at nightfall, Samuel Adams and some of his fellow radicals, some dressed as American Indians, boarded the three ships and began throwing their cargo of 342 containers of tea into the harbor.

For the next few months, the radical Patriots were fairly quiet. The Sons of Liberty, and other patriotic groups, were still agitated for more freedom from London. While they stayed active in their public postings and meetings in town squares, the violence between the colonists and English soldiers were at a minimum.

However, England was still wary of the ruffians from Boston, and Parliament was determined to get payment for the tea dumped into the harbor.

Parliament believed that the best way to handle the increasingly riotous Bostonians was to intimidate and coerce them into obedience. Or, at least, that was the plan.

On March 25, 1774, Parliament passed the Coercive Acts, known as the "Intolerable Acts" by the American colonists. The Coercive Acts actually consisted of four parts. The first part was the Boston Port Act. The other three were the Quartering Act, the Massachusetts Government Act, and the Administration of Justice Act. The purpose of the Boston Port Act was to shut down all commercial shipping in Boston harbor until Massachusetts paid for all of the tea it had destroyed.

The passing of the Coercive Acts rekindled the colonists' fury toward Parliament. Samuel Adams and other leaders of the Sons of Liberty held a town meeting on May 12, which called for a boycott of English goods imported into America.

On May 13, General Thomas Gage, the commander of the British forces in America, replaced Hutchison as the Royal Governor of Massachusetts. Within days, his authority was reinforced by the arrival of four regiments of British troops. With this turn of events, colonists realized martial law was just a step away.

By May 20, England put the next series of Coercive Acts into effect which were the Massachusetts Government Acts and the Administration of Justice Act. When enacted, the Massachusetts Government Act revoked the colonies' charter and would place most of the governmental authority in the Royal Governor. The citizens of Massachusetts would no longer be able to elect persons to government posts. The crown would fill all of the positions. Massachusetts would then be under martial law.

The Administration of Justice Act was an attempt to end self-rule by the colonists. It also banned prosecution of any English official by the colonists. Also imposed, was the Quebec Act, which extended the southern borders of Canada into the colonies of Massachusetts, Connecticut, and Virginia.

In June 1774, in spite of the agitation between the colonies and Britain, David was elected, along with Ben Franklin, Dr. Smith, and Dr. Rush, as a corresponding member of the Virginia Society for Promoting Useful Knowledge. The invitation to join the Society came from its most powerful member, John Page. The Virginia Society was short lived and fairly unproductive. However, it did provide David with valuable introductions.

June also found David attending the meeting of the radical Philadelphia Mechanics Association in State House Square. Approximately 1,200 mechanics from the area were in attendance. At the meeting, a resolution was passed calling for support of the formation of a new Continental Congress. Also, the Association formed its own Committee of Correspondence.

Because of David's reputation for honesty and integrity, he was the first one appointed to the committee. His first assignment was to answer a communication the Philadelphians had received from the mechanics of New York.

The appointment enabled David to become one of the most distinguished mechanics in the city and to establish a strong political base. Someone even named their privately-owned ship, the "Rittenhouse."

Within days of David's appointment, General Gage sealed the ports of Boston and Charlestown with the aid of the British Navy. Merchants became afraid that the blockade would lead to their financial ruin. Many of them began to call for payment of the tea and the demobilization of the Boston Committee of Correspondence.

However, at a town meeting called specifically to discuss the merchants' fears, their fellow citizens displayed little regard for the merchants. Non-merchants almost unanimously voted against resolutions presented by the merchants.

When Parliament passed the Coercive Acts, it hoped that it could isolate Boston, Massachusetts and the whole of New England from the rest of the colonies. But rather than forsake Boston, their necessities were supplied by the other colonies.

On September 5, delegates from most of the other colonies met in Carpenters Hall in Philadelphia and convened the first Continental Congress. The Congress was in session until October 26. Its first act was a declaration of opposition to the Coercive Acts and a call for public disobedience to it.

On October 14, the Continental Congress voiced its opposition to not only the Coercive Acts, but also, the Québec and any other acts which would infringe on America's self-rule. The Congress left no doubt of the rights of Americans, including the rights to life, liberty, and enjoyment of property.

On October 20, the Congress adopted the Continental Association, advocating the boycott of English goods and an embargo on all exports to Britain. At the urging of Anthony Benezet, who had founded the Society for the Relief of Free Negroes Unlawfully Held in Bondage, the Continental Congress agreed to the suspension of the slave trade.

David was appointed engineer to the Continental Association's Committee of Safety on October 27. As its engineer, David became involved in a subcommittee of merchants, iron masters, and army officers seeking better ways to produce gunpowder and armaments, especially the casting of heavy cannon.

The Christmas of 1774 was the last Christmas the Rittenhouse family would have in relative peace for quite some time. David knew that the probability of war with Britain was higher than it had ever been. If this was going to be the last quiet Christmas for a while, David wanted to share it with his family where he had experienced so many other great Christmases, at his old family homestead in Norriton.

He and his family stayed in Norriton for about three weeks before returning to Philadelphia. During those three weeks, David was reminded of the times his mother would tell him that his sickness was caused by his need to study continuously and constantly work. Therefore, he dedicated those three weeks to his family, rest, and relaxation.

When he returned to Philadelphia, he was asked to deliver a speech on the behalf of the Society on the History of Astronomy.

While David was preparing his speech, the relationship between America and Parliament deteriorated rapidly.

On February 1, a Massachusetts provincial congress directed John Hancock, Dr. Joseph Warren, and Dr. Benjamin Church to begin defensive preparations for a state of war.

On February 9, Parliament declared Massachusetts to be in a state of rebellion.

On February 21, Provincial Congress appointed Dr. Church and Dr. Warren as a committee to make an inventory of medical supplies necessary for the army.

David's speech on February 24, 1775, was not as fiery as Patrick Henry's "Give me liberty or give me death", given in Virginia a month later, but to the people of Philadelphia who greatly admired David and his accomplishments, it was just as memorable.

David delivered his speech in a weakened voice but spoke with words that were plainly understood by even the scientifically uninitiated. His words that delivered his message were well thought out, well researched, and vibrantly presented.

His oration, though an account of the history and the current status of astronomy, was also an insight into David's inner thoughts on religion, philosophy, the future of astronomy and his concerns for the future of the country.

Over 150 people crammed into a hall at the University of Philadelphia to hear David's speech. Those in attendance included the governor, the speaker, members of the assembly, as well several members of the Society, and those citizens fortunate to have purchased tickets well in advance.

In presenting his views on the history of astronomy, he criticized the thought that astronomy grew from astrology. He believed it was the other way around. He spoke of Copernicus, who, he said, "explained the true nature of the universe" in defiance of Aristotelian. He openly admitted his admiration for Isaac Newton. And while all of the thoughts and discoveries of Roger Bacon, Tyco Brahe, Johannes Kepler, and Galileo Galilei were important, a basic element of truth was missing from their work.

"And it was, I make no doubt, by a particular appointment of Providence that at this time the immortal Newton appeared." It was Newton who discovered the glue that put all of the thoughts before him in harmony. By discovering the laws of motion, and governing all motion of all celestial bodies, even their irregular ones, he reduced them to their "most beautiful simplicity." Together with his discovering the principles of gravity, Newton founded a philosophy that "will be as durable as science, and can never sink into neglect, until 'universal darkness buries us all.'"

During his speech he openly admitted his belief in God and often spoke of God as Creator, divine architect, the divinity, and the Almighty Power. And while he never spoke of God as a Redeemer, he did express a belief, as he had on many occasions before, and would also do on his death bed, that life after death was a future state of punishments or rewards.

Further, he believed that "true religion" and "true science" were parallel and at some point in the future, those truths would blend because there can only be one truth. He also expressed his belief that there may be inhabitants on other planets. He envisioned those inhabitants as free from the depravity that cursed those of us on earth.

He was particularly vehement toward those who would keep other humans as slaves. Both he and his brother, Benjamin, employed Negro servants, but slavery was something he truly abhorred.

> *"None of your sons and daughters, degraded from their native dignity, have been doomed to endless slavery by us in America, merely because their bodies may be disposed to reflect or absorb the rays of light, in a way different from ours."*

On March 30, 1775, King James endorsed the New England Restraining Act. The new law prohibited the New England colonies from trading with any country except England and also [forbids] forbade fishing in the North Atlantic.

Since late 1773, Paul Revere, a 40-year-old silversmith, and self-taught dentist had served as Boston's Committee of Public Safety courier, carrying the news between New York, Philadelphia, and Boston. It was with his help that the chain of events in Massachusetts, most particularly in Boston, did not escape the notice of the other colonies.

By May 17, 1775, colonists in New York and Philadelphia were calling for a meeting of representatives from all of the colonies to form a colonial congress to discuss ways to combat the Coercive Acts. It was the result of one of Revere's rides to pass information to the Philadelphia Committee of Safety's Committee of Correspondence, that David became acquainted with Revere. They quickly became good friends.

In addition to being an "express" for the Committee of Public Safety, Revere made anti-British engravings. The *Royal American Magazine*, a monthly Patriot magazine, published most of his engravings. He was also one of the leaders of the "Boston Tea Party." David often confessed his admiration for Revere's dedication to, and inexhaustible zeal for, the patriotic cause.

After the Coercive Acts had passed, Revere and a group of 30 other mechanics began holding secret meetings in a local pub called the *Green Dragon*. One of the purposes of the meetings was to provide and coordinate the gathering and dissemination of intelligence by close surveillance of the movement of British soldiers.

With rebellion becoming more and more possible, Parliament ordered Governor Gage to enforce the Coercive Acts, and to use any means necessary to quash "open rebellion" by the colonists. But rather than quash the open rebellion, Governor Gage incited the rebels even more.

On April 7, after observing British military activity that suggested the potential movement of troops, Dr. Joseph Warren, a close friend of Revere, sent him to warn the Massachusetts Provincial Congress, then located in Concord. Concord was also the site of one of the major caches of the patriots' military supplies. After hearing the warning from Revere, the residents began moving the cache of weapons out of town.

A week later, Parliament ordered Gage to disarm the rebels and to imprison Samuel Adams and John Hancock. Four days later, Dr. Warren had learned that British troops were headed for Lexington and Concord in an attempt to capture Adams and Hancock. Warren and his cohorts dismissed any thoughts about the troops moving to capture the Patriots' arsenal in Concord because they thought to be safe.

Thinking that it was Lexington that was in danger, Warren sent Revere and William Dawes to warn rebel leaders in Lexington as well as alert colonial militias along the way.

The British troops, according to the rebels' intelligence a few days earlier, were possibly going by boat from Boston to Cambridge and then to Lexington. It was also possible they were going to make the trip by land.

Therefore, Revere had made arrangements to have the colonists in Charleston alerted of troop movements as they became known by way of the lanterns in the steeple of the North Church. If the troops were moving by water across the Charles River, five lanterns would shine from the steeple. If the troop movements were by land, one lantern would shine from the steeple. After slipping by a British warship anchored in the Charleston River, Revere landed in Charleston by rowboat, and from there he rode to Lexington. Using stealth, Revere was able to avoid a British patrol and continued his ride, warning almost every house along the route that "The Regulars are coming out." Many of those he alerted set out on horseback to deliver warnings of their own.

After meeting with Samuel Adams, and John Hancock in Lexington after midnight, they continued to Concord, accompanied by Dr. Samuel Prescott. Along the way, the trio was accosted by a British patrol that had made a roadblock. Both Dawes and Prescott escaped capture. Revere, however, was captured, only to be freed a few hours later. He was able to make his way back to the Clarke house where Adams and Hancock were staying.

At dawn the next morning, about 70 armed Massachusetts militiamen stood face-to-face on Lexington Green with British advance guard. The British troops were shouting insults and instructions to get out of the way at the militiamen. The militiamen were shouting insults and rebel slogans at the British.

In the midst of all of the shouting, a shot rang out. The Revolutionary War that would change the world had begun! A hail of British rifle fire and a charge with bayonets followed that single shot. After the melee had subsided, eight Americans were left dead, and ten others were wounded.

The British then advanced on to the weapons depot in Concord where they destroyed the colonists' cache. Another battle ensued at Northridge in Concord when the Patriots attacked a British platoon. Two more colonists perished along with 12 British soldiers.

Word of the skirmishes quickly made their way to David and his Committee of Correspondence in Philadelphia. When he informed Barton of the battles that had ensued in Lexington and Concord, Barton was obviously concerned for those Americans, such as himself, who had expressed loyalty to the Crown.

"And now what is to become of us who denounce this 'march to independence' as tomfoolery?" Barton said, throwing his hands in the air in disgust.

"What about us who feel no grievance toward the Crown or Parliament? Are we to be treated as though we're not present, even though this land is as much ours as it is yours? Are we to stand by and let your ruffians trample on all that we have built over the last 200 years or more? We are Americans, as well as they.

"I bear no malice toward you, Davie, you know that, and I disdain the thought of you having ill spite toward me. I know that will never be. But what about the others? How will we be dealt with just because we do not agree with them?"

"As long as none of those who feel like you do not bear arms against those of us seeking to regress our grievances, I'm sure no harm would come to them. And you know I would give my life rather than see harm come to you or my beloved sister."

"It is still my hope, as well as the hope of all good men that I know, that reconciliation with Britain and America is in the future while achieving the independence of America without further bloodshed, and all will end well."

As for Barton, he still believed that the "ruffians" that stirred up all of the trouble would not look kindly on citizens who favored obedience to British rule rather than rebellion against it. Secretly he had made contingency plans for an escape to Canada if need be.

David's hope for independence without further bloodshed was short lived. Soon after the battles of Lexington and Concord, a troop of approximately 13,000 colonials surrounded British-occupied Boston in a siege. However, it was soon realized by the Americans that they did not have sufficient munitions to carry on the siege.

The Massachusetts Committee of Safety formulated a plan to capture Fort Ticonderoga, which by now had become dilapidated with disuse.

However, it still contained a large amount of arms and ammunition, including cannons.

Benedict Arnold was commissioned by the Provincial Congress of Massachusetts, and given the rank of Colonel. He was to advance to the fort with 400 men and to capture the desperately needed weaponry.

Almost simultaneously, the colony of Connecticut developed a similar plan calling for the "Green Mountain Boys" led by Colonel Ethan Allen to capture the fort. After some dispute between Allen and Arnold regarding leadership, it was decided they would co- command their combined forces.

At daybreak on May 10, without a single shot fired, they slipped into the fort and captured it. They confiscated ammunition, cannons, and gunpowder. The cannons were mounted on wagons and pulled by oxen to Boston.

Shortly after the siege of Boston began, Dr. Benjamin Church, a well-known and well-respected member of the Massachusetts Provincial Congress, met with the second Continental Congress in Philadelphia to discuss the defense of Massachusetts. Earlier in the month, on May 12, as the chairman of a subcommittee of the Massachusetts Committee of Safety, he had signed a report, recommending a system of defenses on Prospect Hill and Bunker Hill.

While in Philadelphia, Dr. Church met with David and other members of the Pennsylvania Committee of Correspondence. David cautiously approached the meeting because had earlier received a communication from Paul Revere, warning that he seriously believed Dr. Church might be a spy for the British. Revere, however, had no proof of his allegations.

David was shocked! Dr. Church was well thought of, both as an outstanding surgeon and as a patriot in the struggle against England. Without further proof, David was reluctant to bring the matter before the Committee of Safety.

During the first several days of its existence, the Second Continental Congress was in disarray. Peyton Randolph, the Virginia delegate, who was elected president, but was then called back to Virginia to preside over the House of Burgesses in his home state. Henry Middleton was chosen as a replacement for Randolph. He declined the office, and the Congress elected John Hancock in his place.

There had been no delegate from Georgia, although Lyman Hall attended as a delegate from his local parish in Georgia. It was not until July 8 that Georgia decided to send delegates to the Second Continental Congress. Those delegates did not arrive until July 20.

Without the Georgia delegates present, the Second Continental Congress, on June 14, created the Continental Army, comprised mainly of the troops besieging Boston. The next day it appointed one of the delegates from Virginia, George Washington, to take command of those troops as Commanding General.

David, and some the other members of the Philadelphia Committee of Safety were, during those first few weeks, dubious of the ability of the Continental Congress to properly conduct and oversee the war, if indeed there was to be one. However, when David's good friend, Thomas Jefferson, was appointed as a delegate to replace Peyton Randolph, they felt more reassured.

Before Washington was able to arrive in Cambridge to take command of the troops in Boston, the Patriots had seen indications that the British had designs on occupying Dorchester Heights on the south side of the city. That location was strategically important because it overlooked Boston Harbor, as well as the city itself.

On June 15, about 1,200 American troops from Cambridge, under the direction of Col. William Prescott, dug fortifications on Breeds Hill in an attempt to fortify the area around Bunker Hill. General Gage ordered 4,600 British troops to capture the Patriots' position. Before the British troops could attack, troops from New Hampshire under the direction of Col. John Stark, reinforced Prescott and his men.

After three attempts, the redcoats were able to dislodge the Patriots from their position on Breeds Hill. When the battle was over, the British claimed victory. However, 1,154 dead or wounded were sustained by the Royal forces while the Americans suffered 417 dead or wounded.

Psychologically, the battle of Bunker Hill proved to the Americans that British troops were not invincible, and that the Americans had the ability to win battles against them. The courage of the Americans during the battle also gendered some English sympathy for their cause.

David was one of those patriots who still hoped for a peaceful resolution with England, however, when he heard that the Continental Congress had appointed George Washington as commander in chief of the Continental troops, if they were to engage in an all-out-war with Britain, he felt that the colonials now had a fighting chance. David had the opportunity to meet Washington several years earlier through his brother-in-law, Thomas Barton, who had been Chaplain during the French and Indian War, where Washington was a commissioned major.

As David's fame increased, Washington became more interested in his work, as well as in the man himself. While on the surface, it was a casual relationship, each man felt a deep respect for the other.

After Washington was appointed as Commander in Chief, another appointment by the Continental Congress shortly after, did cause David some concern. On July 27, it authorized the establishment of the Medical Department of the Army with a Director General and Chief Physician.

The Director General-Chief Physician's responsibility was to head up the Hospital Department of the first Army Hospital, as well as the first headquarters of regimental surgeons. Dr. Benjamin Church was chosen to fill that position.

David's concern with Dr. Church proved justified. Shortly after his appointment, Church sent a coded letter addressed to Major Cane, a British officer in Boston. Church's former mistress received the letter, and she entrusted the delivery of the letter to Major Cane to one of her other admirers.

That admirer became suspicious of the letter, but not knowing what to do with it, he held on to it for several weeks. Finally, acting upon the advice of a friend the letter was opened. It was written in code, but the two men were able to decipher it, except for one thing. The author was still unknown.

The admirer immediately it sent to General Washington, who began a search for the spy. While the letter made no disclosures of great importance, it did declare that its author was still loyal to the crown.

Eventually, Church's former mistress was arrested, and under questioning, admitted that her former lover had given her the letter. Dr. Church was eventually arrested and confessed to the letter. He was relieved of his duties on October 17 by the Continental Congress. He was expelled from the Massachusetts Provincial Congress and confined to jail in Connecticut. Revere's suspicions had been proven correct.

In the midst of the hunt for America's first traitor, Washington was also occupied with fighting the war which was not going gloriously for the Patriots. On September 15, the British had landed 4000 troops at Kips Bay in Manhattan. Continental forces made a valiant attempt to keep control of the island but were driven to Harlem Heights in the north end of Manhattan.

On September 16, Washington arrived in Harlem Heights and was greeted by a Continental Army that seemed confused and demoralized. He quickly reassembled the troops in time to stop any further advancement of the British, and, in fact, after flanking the English troops, the Continentals slowly pushed the invaders back. The victory was a huge morale booster for the American troops as well as the citizenry that believed in the Patriots' cause.

By this time, several members of the Rittenhouse family living in the Pennsylvania and New Jersey areas had enlisted in the Continental Army and were in their local militias. David's brother, Benjamin, was involved in the local militia as Captain in Worchester Township, near Norriton.

On September 28, David was asked by the Committee of Safety to view a group of row galleys which were to be shown to the Continental Congress, the Pennsylvania Assembly, and a group of leading citizens. When David boarded the *Bull Dog*, he found himself in the presence of the likes of Owen Biddle, Michael Hillegas, and John Adams. Adams and David struck an almost immediate mutual admiration for each other.

On October 27, the Pennsylvania Assembly named David as the engineer for the Committee of Safety. One of his first duties was to help survey the Delaware River from Marcus Hook to the city, in an attempt to determine the best means of fortifying against the invasion of the city by the river.

A major concern of the Assembly, was the lack of munitions in the Philadelphia area. While local ironmasters were able to make small cannons, the Assembly felt the need for the casting of larger cannons.

David was asked to review the feasibility of entering into a contract with one of two local foundries, one owned by Samuel Potts, and another owned by Morgan Bumstead. After reviewing the facilities with local merchants, iron casters, and military personnel, David advised the committee to enter into an agreement with Potts for the larger cannons.

During the year, John Murray, Earl of Dunmore, who was the Royal Governor of Virginia, had been a thorn in the side of the patriots. The militia, led by Patrick Henry, had been able to drive him and his loyalists out of Williamsburg earlier in the year.

However, after his retreat to Norfolk, Dunmore attempted to rebuild his forces by offering emancipation to any slave of a patriot who would join his troops. Over 800 slaves, nicknamed the "Ethiopian Regiment," took him up on his offer. General Washington, however, was still wary of the capabilities of Dunmore to defeat the patriotic cause in the South. He warned Congress that the sound defeat of Dunmore must be a necessity.

While Dunmore had built his troops to some 600 men, which he believed was sufficient power to retake all of Virginia for the crown. He advanced to Kempts Landing and took control of it. He then fortified his position at Great Bridge, ten miles distance from Kempts Landing.

Meanwhile, Colonel William Woodford, commander of the 2nd Virginia Regiment, was amassing his troops along with Minutemen in the same area. About 150 Patriots from North Carolina joined them. Meeting Dunmore at Great Bridge, the two sides clashed in battle. When it was all over with, there was one patriot fatality and 102 loyalist's fatalities. Those of Dunmore's troops who survived escaped to his ship, the Otter, where most eventually succumbed to smallpox.

Virginia was finally rid of British rule, once and for all. It appeared that the Patriots would close out the year, 1775, on a high note. However, on December 31, the Patriots, led by Benedict Arnold, attempted to liberate Quebec from British control. This battle would be the first defeat for the Americans.

David was fearful the Patriots may have evoked a war they could not win. Still, he was determined to do what he could to ensure an American victory.

CHAPTER 3

"Just who do your rabble-rousing friends think they are?" Barton asked angrily as he burst into David's workshop on January 5, 1776. "They have no right to force their politics on those of us who do not share their radical thinking!" David had never seen his brother-in-law this angry.

"I haven't the slightest idea of what you are speaking about. Who are my rabble-rousing friends, and what have they done to make you so upset?" David asked as he watched Barton pace back and forth.

"Your so-called "Continental Congress" just put out what it calls the 'Tory Banishment Act.' Surely, you know about it as a member of the Safety Committee. You're the one that's supposed to be enforcing this damnable thing."

David shook his head and motioned for Barton to sit down. "Is that it in your hand?" he asked, taking the pamphlet from him. Refusing to sit down Barton angrily tossed the paper in David's direction. David picked it up from the table where it had landed and commenced reading it.

"I don't understand your anger," David said, handing the document back to Barton. "You are not someone of whom this resolution is speaking. It is addressing those Loyalists who would bear arms against the patriotic cause."

"This blasted thing goes beyond that; they want to bully anyone who disagrees with them to take up their side. And if I refuse to do so, I am to be coerced into it."

"Here, here," Barton said as he began scanning the paper, "it says right here that I should be indoctrinated by the likes of rowdies enlightening me to the 'origin, nature and extent of the present controversy.' I am now to be treated as a schoolboy, unschooled in the world swirling about me. I refuse to be treated as an idiot who does not understand what this war, or controversy as they put it, is all about."

"And they want us to give up our arms, whether we have raised them against the rebels or we haven't. They cannot expect us to surrender our guns when they are threatening retaliation if we don't do what they ask or come around to their way of thinking."

David had no response. He did not believe in forcing his political positions on anyone. Persuasion through conversation was one thing. Threatening and coercion were quite another.

Soon after his conversation with Barton, he voiced his opinion to both the Committee of Safety and members of the Continental Congress. He especially made his concerns about the resolution known to his friend Thomas Jefferson.

Jefferson confided to David that he was not in favor of disarming all Tories, just those Tories who had raised arms in defense of the Crown. And, as a matter-of-fact, he believed all Americans should have the right to keep and bear arms.

David took the matter no further, nor did Barton. However, as a consequence of the resolutions, thousands of Tories did abandon America for Canada and Nova Scotia over the next several months. By the war's end, more than 16,000 Loyalists and 20,000 slaves left for other parts of the English Empire.

On January 9, the fiery Irish immigrant, Thomas Paine, published a pamphlet which attacked not only the King but the system of monarchy as well. In his pamphlet, "Common Sense," he stated,

"We have it in our power to begin the world.
The new... America shall make a stand, not for herself alone,
but for the world."

Again David and Barton were on the opposite sides of the debate.

"I can't believe the arrogance and the narcissism involved in this movement to abolish English rule in America. Do you really think that the world gives a pence about what is going on in this struggle?"

"Or, that somehow it is going to make a difference to anyone else but Americans, or that the world will be changed for the better if you get your way?" Barton fulminated to David shortly after the publication of Paine's pamphlet.

"I don't know what's going to happen when this is all over with," David responded. "But I do know that there are millions of people around the world suffering the same fate as us, and some even worse at the hands of monarchs or an elite privileged few.

"Monarchy and other forms of despotism must become relics of the past. It is man's nature to be free to have the liberty to do with his life and his property as he wishes. Whether our struggle will make a difference to the world, I do not know. But I do know that if we are victorious, it will make the difference to Americans."

Barton disagreed, of course, but the two friends, despite their vast political differences, would remain steadfast and loyal to each other until death. It never entered either one of their minds that because they disagreed on so serious a proposition that they would not remain the best of friends.

After David's appointment as engineer to the committee of safety in October of the previous year, he had been asked to serve on several subcommittees. Most of the subcommittees had to do with things in which

David did not have any background or experience. [in.] Many involved the manufacturer of munitions and armament including the manufacture of cannon and saltpeter.

By January, David had become an expert on explosives and rifles. He even experimented with rifling the barrel of a cannon. He and Charles Willson Peale conducted several experiments with rifles, including developing telescopic sights and equipping the stock of rifles with boxes large enough to carry ammunition.

On January 19, David was appointed to the cannon committee to oversee the production of the cannon by the Potts factory. Then, on January 22, he was given the assignment, along with Samuel Morris Jr., John McNeil, and Daniel Joy, of surveying the Jersey shoreline from Billingsport to Newtown Creek, in an attempt to locate the best spots for building fortifications on the far shore.

He knew that the basic plan was to sink obstacles in the river which would prohibit British ships from invading from downstream. This plan would be effective only if the Americans had barricades strategically placed along the river to constantly harass British ships with cannon fire.

After completing the survey, David's committee determined that building any kind of barrier was not the best strategy because it would take a superior army to prevent British landings above or below their effort, and if British captured a newly constructed fort, the fort could then be used against the Americans.

Instead, they advised the employment of a mobile defense which would include several 12 or 18 cannons mounted on strong moving platforms, mounted behind breastworks which would be at previously constructed sites. This would give the Americans some ability to harass the British at several locations and to give them the ability to retreat quickly, if necessary.

After inspecting the ground with his staff for a few months, General Washington vetoed the committee's recommendation. Washington did not believe that untrained American forces had the mobility to carry out David's plan.

At the end of January 1776, the Committee of Safety had decided to establish a gun lock factory. David's brother, Benjamin, was chosen to be superintendent of the factory. In a letter to Benjamin, the committee informed him of his duties, and they would include to employ immediately as many people as possible. The committee was sure "a number of ingenious and handy black and white smiths, may soon be instructed and at several parts."

On February 16, Benjamin wrote to the committee that he would take the job if paid £250, plus £50 in case his employment ended before three years. However, his duties as captain of a company of militia in Norristown commanded his attention until the end of February, when he finally became a superintendent of the Philadelphia Gun Lock Factory.

In late February, Benjamin Franklin resigned his seat in the Pennsylvania Assembly, stating he was too old to retain the seat, and to fulfill his duties as a delegate to the Continental Congress. On March 2, in a special election, David was elected to fulfill Franklin's unexpired term in the Assembly.

In this capacity, David was fully prepared to back any resolutions or laws favoring declaring independence from England. However, the majority in the Assembly were not so inclined.

At that point, the war seemed to be going in the Patriots' favor, especially for those troops surrounding Boston. On March 4, General Washington had instructed Brigadier General John Thomas to take 800 soldiers and 1,200 workers to Dorchester Heights, covertly and under the cover of darkness, and begin securing the area. American cannons, located at another location, began a noisy bombardment on the outskirts of the city to cover the sound of the construction.

General William Howe had planned to destroy the American's position with the British ships in Boston Harbor, but a storm set in, giving the Americans enough time to complete the fortifications and set up their artillery.

Realizing their position was now indefensible, 11,000 British troops and some 1,000 Loyalists departed Boston by ship on March 17, sailing to the safety of Halifax, Nova Scotia, thus ending eight years of hated British occupation of Boston. Congress awarded its first ever medal to General Washington as his reward for the victory.

On March 14, Alexander Hamilton received his commission as captain of a New York artillery company. A year later, after Hamilton had established himself as an outstanding military leader, he came to the attention of General Washington, who commissioned him Lieutenant Colonel, and made him his personal aide.

On April 6, 1776, the Pennsylvania Assembly adjourned until May 20th, the date of elections for the newly created seats. Prior to its adjournment, the Assembly had added four more seats from Philadelphia and two more seats to five back-country counties as well as one seat to three other back-country counties.

The elections for the new seats did not go well for David and other radicals in the Assembly. They did not win the majority they had hoped, and the Continental Congress became more convinced that the hesitancy of the existing government of Pennsylvania was the main blockage to declaring independence.

The pressure on Pennsylvania to back independence became even greater, when on May 4, Rhode Island became the first colony to vote for independence from the British government.

On May 10, John Adams introduced a resolution stating that "the respective Assemblies and Conventions of the United colonies, where no government sufficient to the exigencies of their affairs have been made hitherto established, to adopt such government as, in the opinion of the representatives of the people best conduce to the happiness and safety of their constituents in particular, and America in general."

In May, things began to happen rapidly for the Patriots. French King Louis XVI promised to support the rebellion by supplying $1 million in arms and munitions to the rebels, and the Continental Congress authorized privateer raids on British ships. In addition, Spain offered support to the Americans. On May 10, the Continental Congress authorized the formation of provincial governments.

Then, on June 7, Richard Henry Lee, Virginia's delegate to the Continental Congress, presented a formal resolution calling for America to declare independence from Britain. Tabling the resolution until July, on June 11, the Congress appointed a committee to draft a Declaration of Independence, consisting of Thomas Jefferson, Benjamin Franklin, John Adams, Roger Livingston and Roger Sherman. Thomas Jefferson was appointed to make the first draft.

Meanwhile, Adams' resolution created a polarization of the political factions for and against independence. At a public meeting in the Pennsylvania State House yard, the majority of the four or five thousand people gathered preferred the formation of a new government for Pennsylvania. That, however, did not mean they favored independence.

Finally, on June 18, Pennsylvania's Assembly instructed its delegates to the Continental Congress to "concur" with other delegations. The assembly was cautious, however, not to include the word "independence" in its instructions. At the same time, a conference of Provincial Committees met in Philadelphia and set July 8 as the date for electing delegates to the state constitutional convention.

This effectively passed the argument on to the Pennsylvania delegates to the second Continental Congress, the majority of which was resisting the move toward independence, and hence, to Congress itself.

On July 2, Congress voted for independence. On July 4, it formally endorsed Jefferson's Declaration, written on fine parchment. Copies, printed on Rittenhouse paper, were sent to all the colonies.

On the evening of July 7, Thomas Jefferson visited with David and Benjamin and their families. Jefferson suggested that David should take Benjamin's wife Elizabeth and his wife, Hannah to the second floor of the State House to Hear the reading of the Declaration of Independence the next day.

Fortunately, July 8 was a warm and sunny day. It had rained on July 7, and the rumbling of thunder rolled across the early morning skies. A large crowd gathered in the State House and its yard in Philadelphia to hear the reading of the Declaration as the ceremonies began.

David was in conflict on whether to file into the State House with the representatives of the Philosophical Society as its president or with the representatives of the Committee of Safety, which was the most important of the two. Those in attendance at the reading were also there to vote for delegates to the state's constitutional convention.

About noon, the bell in the State House tower began to peal, and those who gathered on the main floor started to part, making way for the procession dignitaries. The Committee of Inspection was the first to enter, and then came David with the Committee of Safety. Then the Congressional doors were opened, and the members of Congress took their positions.

As the proclamation was read many of the people were so moved by the occurrence they wept. The words were grand and glorious and inspired the many of them, who until this point were torn between the revolution and the crown, to favor the revolution.

After the Declaration was read, a hush settled over the crowd. Then suddenly there was a tremendous roar from the crowd. The Statehouse bell began to ring again, followed by the bells of the St. Peter's Christ Church and Gloria Dei. Those favoring it, erupted in impromptu parades, the ringing of bells and even bonfires. Inside the Assembly and courtroom, emblems representing the crown were ripped from the walls.

Of course, not everyone was happy. Many people, mostly Tories, did not believe that this was a sensible course for America to follow. To some, David's association with the Patriots was an assurance of its wisdom. To others, it represented not only a national tragedy but a personal tragedy for David, as well. As one poet put it:

Oblivion shall entomb thy name,
and from the Roles of future fame,

---

thou'll fall, to rise no more.
Labor not in State Affairs
keep acquaintance with Stars
for there thy Genius lies.

David was also elected as a member of the Pennsylvania State Constitutional Convention on that day. Writing a new state constitution that was acceptable to the majority was going to be difficult, since those who felt the need for it were in a minority.

Another problem the convention faced was that the delegates were, for the most part, unknown and untrained in government. Dissenters of the delegates to the Constitutional Convention were reminded that both Benjamin Franklin and David Rittenhouse were delegates.

David's name was not as illustrious as Ben Franklin's, but it possessed a resiliency that resisted the persistent defamation of that era. Even the most sincere dissenters never thought to try to mar the icon that David had become.

David found that many delegates to the convention were men "who would go to the devil for popularity." David's presence at the convention was important mostly because the people felt he would not succumb to any principles other than his own. They knew his thoughts were to put the government in the hands of the wisdom and virtue of the average citizen.

No one's presence on the committee that formed the Pennsylvania Constitution of 1776 was more visible than David's. He was on the committee that prepared the declaration of rights and even chaired that committee at one point. He was on the committee that prepared the preamble to the Constitution and the oath of office and the committee on style. No other member took part in every single phase of the production of the Constitution.

On August 2, the parchment copy of the Declaration of Independence was formally signed. America was now in a battle for its very existence.

About that time, General Washington communicated to Major-General Charles Lee that the Continental Army's situation had deteriorated due to an outbreak of smallpox and desertion. It was Washington's fear that the British Navy might blockade and isolate New York from communicating with other states.

If Washington were correct, the British would capture New York City, thereby controlling the Hudson River, dividing the colonies in half. General William Howe and his army landed on Long Island on August 22. On August 27, they rushed the Patriot position at Brooklyn Heights, defeating the Americans at Gowanus Pass, before outflanking Washington's entire army. The Americans ended up suffering heavy casualties.

Fortunately, Howe did not listen to his subordinate's advice to advance on the Patriot positions at Brooklyn Heights. If he had done so, he may have been able to take the Patriots' military leaders prisoner, or killed them, thereby ending the rebellion.

General Howe and his brother, Admiral Richard Howe, who still sought to convince the Americans to rejoin the British Empire, felt that in the face of the overwhelming defeat, this was a better tactic than forcing the former colonies into submission after executing Washington and his officers as traitors.

On September 11, Benjamin Franklin, John Adams, and other Congressional representatives reopened negotiations with the Howe brothers on Staten Island. However, they were unsuccessful because the British refused to accept the idea of American independence. The British captured New York City on September 15.

Philadelphians feared that their city would be the next to be invaded by the British Army. Months ago, after David's surveying expedition to the Delaware River, they had begun to shut off the river from enemy navigation.

However, nothing had been done on the fortifications since August. David and the Council of Safety needed authorization from the Congressional Board of War to complete the project. On September 16,

David's plea to the Board was granted. His brother Benjamin's father-in-law, John Bull, was chosen to supervise the construction.

In October, it was necessary to find a way to fix a boom and heavy chain across the main river channel to two piers already erected. Once again, the task fell to David. David was also asked to head a committee to reconnoiter all possible land approaches to the city and determine the best place to build fortifications.

David, realizing that fortifications were only useful if you had well-led troops to man them, sought support from the Continental Congress to get some troops stationed near Philadelphia under the command of an experienced general.

In the wake of the defeat in New York and the loss of troops to desertion or sickness, the Congress was unable to respond favorably to David's request.

On November 2, William Demont, an officer under the command of Colonel Robert McGaw, deserted his post at Fort Washington, located on the northern end and the highest point of Manhattan Island. Making his way to General Howe's headquarters, he furnished Howe with the information he needed to overrun the fort.

On November 16, under the command of Hessian Lieutenant General Wilhelm von Knyphausen, a force of 3,000 Hessian mercenaries and 5,000 British troops lay siege on the fort. At first, the American riflemen inside the fort were able to stifle the attack, but by the afternoon, the Americans were overwhelmed.

John and Margaret Corbin of Virginia were among the patriots defending the fort. John had been manning a cannon, and Margaret was helping clean and load John's cannon. When her husband was mortally wounded, Margaret took over his position, cleaning, loading and firing the weapon, until she too fell. Severely wounded in her left arm, she survived the battle but loss the use of her limb. She was the first woman to fight for the Continental Army.

McGaw was forced to surrender. Two thousand eight hundred and eighteen patriots were taken prisoner and were forced to march through the streets of New York, where they were mocked and jeered by the pro-British New Yorkers. Knyphausen also captured valuable ammunition and supplies.

On November 19, Congress sent a plea to the states to send more soldiers, reminding them "how indispensable it is to the common safety, that they pursue the most immediate and vigorous measures to furnish their respective quotas of Troops for the new army, as the time of service for which the present army was enlisted, is so near expiring."

At the time, Fort Washington was being laid siege to, General Washington was witnessing the battle from across the river at Fort Lee, just above Burdette's landing. Fort Lee and Fort Washington were built at the same time on opposite sides of the Hudson River in an effort to seal off the river. Once Washington realized that Fort Washington had succumbed to the British, he knew he must abandon Fort Lee.

The week before abandoning the fort, Washington had been kept informed of the anticipated movements of the British Army by sixteen-year-old Peter Bourdette, who would row back and forth across the Hudson River gathering intelligence for Washington. Young Bourdette had also rowed Washington to the middle of the river for a strategy session with his officers in charge of New York, who had also rowed out to meet him the night before the battle of Fort Washington.

On the night of November 19, some 5000 British troops were ferried across the Hudson to commence their invasion of New Jersey. But, George Washington and Nathanael Greene had ordered the fort evacuated on November 20.

On Nov 30, with Westchester, Manhattan and Long Island securely in British hands, Admiral Richard Howe and his brother, General William Howe, issued a proclamation from New York City, promising pardon to those who would subscribe within 60 days to a declaration that they would desist from "Treasonable Actings and Doings." Thousands of residents from downstate New York accepted the Howes' offer.

On December 3, General Washington wrote to Congress from his headquarters in Trenton, New Jersey, informing them that he had transported much of the Continental Army's stores and baggage across the Delaware River to Pennsylvania. Washington then confiscated and burned all the boats along the Delaware to prevent British troops from pursuing his beleaguered troops across the river.

On December 11, the Continental Congress, worried about a possible British attack, abandoned Philadelphia.

"My Lord, David, do you realize what this means?" Barton asked when he heard the news. David looked at him with a quizzical look on his face. "It means I will be moving back to Norriton, or Lancaster until the threat has passed. What do you think it means?" David replied.

"It means that your beautiful orreries are in danger of being confiscated and sent back to England, or even worse, God forbid, destroyed," Barton replied anxiously, almost shouting his words at David.

"If they are to be preserved for the enlightenment of mankind, God will see to it that they are preserved," David said quietly.

David and Thomas Jefferson had been in constant correspondence with each other concerning matters of government and the progress of the war. In one letter toward the end of the year, Jefferson even voiced his concern to David that perhaps the Americans should cease their fight.

In another letter, David questioned Jefferson about the phrase in the Declaration of Independence which states all men are created equal. David saw the phrase as a contradiction to the practice of slavery.

Jefferson pointed out to David that slaves were property, and by many, were not considered human. He also confided to David that he would have no problem with the abolition of slavery, but he feared that if the thousands of Negroes now held as slaves were freed, they might rebel against their former masters.

On December 25, Washington crossed the Delaware River to conduct a surprise raid the next day on 1,500 Hessian troops at Trenton. After an hour's battle, the Hessians surrendered and Washington's army took some 1,000 prisoners. The Americans' only casualties were four dead and six wounded. Washington surrounded and reoccupied Trenton. The victory boosted the morale of the American Patriots to the point that many believed that victory might very well be theirs in 1777.

Washington knew otherwise. The enlistment of most of his troops ran out on December 31. If he could not convince them to stay at least another month, he knew the fight for freedom and independence would be over.

At first, he simply asked any men who wanted to volunteer to serve when their enlistment ended to poise their firelocks. When men declined to step forward, Washington wheeled his horse around and rode in front of the troops.

"My brave fellows, you have done all I asked you to do and more than could be reasonably expected; but your country is at stake, your wives, your houses and all that you hold dear. You have worn yourselves out with fatigues and hardships, but we know not how to spare you. If you will consent to stay only one month longer, you will render that service to the cause of liberty and to your country which you probably never can do under any other circumstances."

At first, no one broke rank and stepped forward, but then one soldier stepped forward, and one by one, he was followed by most of the others, leaving only a few in the original line. This was perhaps Washington's most essential victory of the year.

CHAPTER 4

Washington's weary troops barely had time to rest and recuperate from their victory on December 26, before British General Charles Cornwallis arrived in Trenton on January 2, with 8,000 troops.

Washington knew that his 5,000 troops, made up of militia, as well as Continentals, were in no condition to face the overwhelming British contingent. Cornwallis knew that Washington was going to retreat, but he could only guess at Washington's route. Thinking that Washington would re-cross the Delaware River, Cornwallis sent some of his troops to guard the river.

Washington, however, had other plans. He left a small band of men behind to tend to multiple campfires and make noises simulating noises coming from a large encampment, while he muscled wagon wheels and silently snuck around the British camp. Those that Washington left behind, caught up with the regular troops by dawn, and they all headed north together. They soon crossed paths with a straggling British rear guard consisting of about 1,000 men.

The ensuing battle, known as the Battle of Princeton, cost the British 275 of their troops. Forty patriots gave their lives for the cause. However, the real result of the battle was that Washington was able to take control of New Jersey.

David, who had been actively communicating to fellow Pennsylvanians and, in circular letters, to commanders of the Pennsylvania battalions, felt some relief over the New Jersey victories.

It was he who had tried to encourage the people of Philadelphia after Washington's defeats in late 1776. Addressing a crowd on November 27, he stated, *"It Is our duty to inform you that our enemies are advancing upon us and that the most vigorous measures alone can save the city from falling into their hands. There is no time for delay, and by your contact, the Continent will be influenced. We, therefore, entreat you, by the most sacred of all bonds-the love of virtue, liberty, and of your country--to forget every distinction, and unite as one man in this time of extreme danger. Let us defend ourselves like men determined to be free."*

He then presided at a mass meeting held in the State House yard the next day. The meeting was attended by a huge number of citizens, as well as all the members of the Council and the Assembly.

He shared the intelligence at hand with the crowd and informed them that it was the expectation that Howe would invade Pennsylvania. He then informed them that several counties were supplying militia to march to New Jersey.

After David's address and closing remarks by the quartermaster General of the Continental Army, Thomas Messing, the crowd broke into cheers and patriotic slogans.

Now, with the victories in New Jersey, he knew that while the war still had a way to go, and victory was still in doubt, the morale of the patriots had been rekindled.

Matters in the Pennsylvania colony, however, were still major concerns for David. He fought for a new State Constitution and a new government. Just as those things were almost achieved, those who were disinfected with the new State Constitution and the State government brought the State Assembly to a standstill. As a result, with a few exceptions, the Assembly was never able to acquire a quorum necessary for meetings.

One of those exceptions was on December 13, 1776, when the Assembly appointed a committee to recover the State Treasury from Baltimore. On October 4, 1776, Pennsylvanian's then Secretary of the Treasury, Michael Hillegas, was appointed Treasurer of the Continental Congress.

When Congress vacated Philadelphia, Hillegas, who was still acting as the Treasurer for Philadelphia, took with him the State's Treasury as well as the Treasury of the Continental Congress. David helped make arrangements for the transfer of the State's Treasury back to Philadelphia, which was completed on December 13, 1776.

On January 13, 1777, the Pennsylvania Assembly once again was able to muster a quorum. The following day it unanimously elected David as the State Treasurer. David now had a dual role as State Treasurer and Vice-Chairman of the Council of Safety under Thomas Wharton, Jr.

Pennsylvania, however, was not the only colony in turmoil. On January 15, 1777, the Green Mountain Boys, along with others residing in the New Hampshire Grants area between the colonies of New York and New Hampshire, held a convention declaring the area was now independent of both colonies, as well as Great Britain. They temporarily named the independent state, New Connecticut.

The war was not going much better than Pennsylvania politics. In the middle of January, the patriots, under the command of Washington, were engaged by Howe in New Jersey. Washington, believing that an attack on Fort Independence in New York would cause Howe to divert some of the troops attacking him to defend the fort, ordered General Heath and his men to begin a siege of the fort. The siege did not go well, mainly because of the weather, and by January 29 Heath was forced to abandon the effort.

Meanwhile, on March 13, the Pennsylvania Supreme Executive Council abolished the Counsel of Safety, replacing it with a new agency called the Board of War. This agency was created to superintend military matters. It was second in power only to the Executive Council. David was the first member elected to the Board.

The loyalty to the new state government was divided mainly between a new Republican Club that was determined to force a new constitutional convention, and the Whig Club, which favored the current constitution and the government established under it. Charles Wilson Peale was the President of the newly formed Whig Club. David, as well as Thomas Paine and others, served on the club's membership committee.

As a result, turmoil continued to reign in Pennsylvania. That disruption was beginning to fester like a blister under the skin of the Continental Congress. Matters had gotten so bad, that on March 7, John Adams, writing to his wife Abigail, declared that Philadelphia had *"lost its vibrancy during congresses removal to Baltimore. This City is a dull Place, in Comparison of what it was. More than one-half of the inhabitants have removed to the Country, as it was their Wisdom to do-the Remainder are chiefly Quakers as dull as Beetles"*.

On April 14, the Continental Congress attempted to exert its influence by requesting that Thomas Wharton, Jr., newly elected President of Pennsylvania, call to order the executive and legislative authorities of the state in order to meet any present war threat.

It was a task that Wharton found to be impossible. Instead, he, David and three other members of the Board of War met with a committee from Congress. All agreed that the present government had been immobilized by the conflict between the Republicans and the Whigs. It was apparent to everyone that the Republicans had achieved their goal. After much posturing by both parties, a referendum on a constitutional convention was scheduled for October.

On June 14, David was given what was perhaps his highest honor. Congress adopted a resolution that "the flag of the United States be 13 alternate stripes red and white." They also ordained, "the Union be at 13 stars, white in a blue field representing a new constellation". Many in America believed "representing a new constellation" was a tribute to David and the honor he had brought to the colonies through his orreries and world-renowned astronomical observations.

By now, the American Revolution was affecting French politics. In December 1776, arrangements were made for 19-year-old Marie-Joseph Paul Roch Yves Gilbert du Motier, Marquis de Lafayette, to come to America, bringing his military expertise with him. The deal was struck by Silas Deane, a delegate to the Continental Congress, on behalf of America.

However, Benjamin Franklin, upon replacing Deane, stifled the deal. As a result, King Louis XVI ordered Lafayette to stay in France. Eventually, Lafayette's ship was seized and the young Marquis was put in prison. Determined to come to America to fight, he managed to escape and, with two British ships pursuing him, he made his way to South Carolina on June 13.

That was about the time that David and Thomas Paine commenced exploring a suggestion by Benjamin Franklin. In the face of a severe shortage of ammunition, Franklin had suggested the use of bows and arrows. At first, the suggestion was not taken seriously, but Paine approached David about the possibility of putting a fire on the tips of the arrows and then coupling them with steel crossbows strong enough to catapult the arrows across the Delaware River.

By July, however, everyone's attention turned to the war and the possible invasion of Philadelphia by either General Howe or General John Burgoyne. It was Howe that most Philadelphians feared would attack their city. It was assumed by everyone that Burgoyne was more interested in concentrating his troops in New York and leaving Philadelphia for Howe.

Howe's intentions became far less clear after he and 15,000 of his men sailed out of Boston Harbor on July 23. Now no one knew if he was going to attack by land or by sea, but Philadelphians were convinced an attack was inevitable.

Howe's ships were seen in Delaware Bay on July 29, but confusion reigned when he turned the ships out to sea. No one had any idea what Howe's next move would be.

Lafayette eventually made his way to Philadelphia from South Carolina, where he met with David and other state politicians. He also met with Congress and offered his services, without pay, to the patriotic colonists. Because of his youth, Congress was reluctant to give him a commission, but because he was willing to serve without pay, he was given a commission as Major-General on July 31.

By August 21, Howe's intentions became much clearer when his ships were reported to be in the Chesapeake. Within two days, Washington had moved his troops through Philadelphia in preparation for meeting Howe south of the city.

With the war approaching, concerns in the city of Philadelphia arose as to who was a loyalist and who supported independence. It was David who had the unfavorable task of deciding who was a Tory and who was a patriot.

On August 31, David, Peale, William Bradford, a descendant of the printer William Bradford, and Sharp Delaney, a Colonel in the Continental Army, were shown a highly secretive resolution of Congress which had been given to the Pennsylvania Supreme Executive Council. The resolution recommended that eleven Quakers be taken into custody and their papers confiscated, due to non-payment of taxes, and being possible spies for the British.

The Council sought the four men's advice concerning other Philadelphians whose names should be part of the list. Eventually, thirty more names were added to those suggested by Congress. One of the names added to that list caused hesitation from David. It was the name of his good friend, Doctor William Smith. After some troubling thought, David finally acquiesced in placing his friend's name on the list, and Doctor William Smith was promptly arrested.

"I implore you, my good friend, to take an oath pledging allegiance to the cause of independence," David begged Smith. Many had been suspicious of Smith even before the outbreak of war.

"As a scientist, I have tried to keep myself above the fray, as I know you had in the beginning. But your ardor for the cause allowed you no hesitation in getting involved in the dispute," Smith replied.

David replied in his usual soft-spoken manner, "My involvement came as a matter of principles. I believe that all men, no matter their race or color, should be free from the overburdening confines of government to choose their God-given course in life."

Personally, David felt a keen appreciation of the plight of those caught in a world of divided loyalties. Several of his own family members, mostly distant relatives, had fled or were preparing to flee to Canada, and Thomas Barton, himself under investigation, fled to New York for the protection of British troops. On the other hand, his brother-in-law, Colonel Caleb Parry, whom David had voted to confirm as a Lieutenant Colonel in March, 1776, died as a patriot in the battle for Long Island on August 28, 1776.

In addition, many of David's family members still followed the Mennonite faith, and as a result were pacifists. This put them in a category John Adams referred to as "a kind of neutral tribe, or the race of the insipids."

David was relieved when Smith summoned him to report that he had relented and was willing to take an oath of loyalty to the free and independent State of Pennsylvania. As a result, Smith was released and placed on parole. Those who did not take the oath were exiled to Winchester and Staunton, Virginia.

The newspapers were in an excited frenzy headlining the atrocities of the British and the exuberance of the Patriots.

When the papers learned of actions taken against Tories, the stories were given the most prominence. Even Tory women did not escape threats of violence.

On September 11, General Howe and General Cornwallis, with a combined contingent of eighteen thousand troops, landed in the Chesapeake Bay. General Washington and the Continental Army, which included Captain Benjamin Rittenhouse, marched through Philadelphia on their way to meet Howe in Wilmington.

David watched the procession with John Adams and others, who remarked that they thought the troops, while lacking the look of a professional army, were more disciplined than ever before and were certainly well-armed and clothed.

After the British landed, they pushed forward in two divisions. Hessian Lieutenant-General Baron Wilhelm Knyphausen led one, while Major-General Cornwallis, who took the lead, led the other. Washington had some of his troops positioned at White Clay Creek, but the main army was guarding the principal route to Philadelphia at the Red Clay Creek, a little west of Newport.

On September 8, Howe had a small force engage the Americans in a frontal attack, while his main army marched around Washington's right flank. Early the next morning, Washington, realizing what Howe was up to, ordered his troops to assemble at Chadds Ford on the Brandywine. Howe, meanwhile, continued to Kennett Square, reaching it on September 10.

Chadds Ford, where the American army now took up positions, was at the point where the Nottingham Road crossed the Brandywine Creek, on the route from Kennett Square to Philadelphia. It was the last natural line of defense before the almost indefensible Schuylkill River.

Washington's main force defended Chadds Ford, and also prepared to prevent possible British flanking movements to the south or north. He then dispatched two brigades of Pennsylvania militia, including Captain Benjamin Rittenhouse's brigade, to Chadds Ford, where Nathaniel Greene's troops made up the main defense. Greene's troops were on either side of Nottingham road going east from the Brandywine.

A mile above Chadds Ford, Major General John Sullivan's 3rd Division took up positions opposite Brenton's Ford. Major General Lord Stirling's 5th Division was held in reserve just behind Sullivan.

Also held in reserve was Major General Adam Stephen's 2d Division, which was in a position to support the right or left of the main body of Washington's army. On the hills on the western side of Chadds Ford, west of the Brandywine, along the Nottingham, Washington positioned a light brigade under the command of Wayne and William Maxwell.

At daybreak on September 11, Howe began moving his army. First, Knyphausen marched with 6,800 men toward Chadds Ford, hoping to keep Washington occupied, while Howe marched northeast from Kennett Square up the Great Valley Road. He then proceeded to cross the Brandywine, going south around the American right flank. He made his moves under cover of a dense fog.

Three miles into his march, Knyphausen encountered Maxwell's men near Welch's Tavern. The Americans took advantage of the thick woods along the road, as they used guerilla tactics mixed with regular volleys for the next several miles. At the hills before Chadds Ford, the patriots emerged from woods and marsh shouting rallying cries, on either side of the road, taking the Tories by surprise.

Artillery on the other side of the Brandywine was firing on the British as well, but because of their poor positioning, this was doing little damage. Some of Greene's men forded the creek to support Maxwell's men who began building breastworks on a hill that overlooked the road on Kyphausen's right.

British riflemen took up positions behind a house while two heavy and two light artillery pieces were moved to a knoll behind them. The English then began bombarding the American breastwork while the infantry drove the Americans from the woods and down to lower land.

By early morning, the British and their allies had cleared the west bank of the Brandywine and occupied a hill overlooking the Ford. Meanwhile, Washington had moved his headquarters to the heights, where a cannon was stationed. From there, he observed the fighting. Washington's main problem now was that he was not getting reliable reports from his commanders. The reports that were coming in were in conflict with one another.

With a detachment of Knyphausen's troops taking positions along the river, Washington could not afford to ignore the possibility of a flanking attack, and sent scouts to reconnoiter the situation.

Washington received a report that Howe's troops seemed to be on their way northeast to Taylor's and Jeffries Ferries on the Brandywine. Washington immediately realized that Howe had split his army and that he may soon be surrounded.

Realizing the danger, Washington determined that an attack on Knyphausen, before Howe had a chance to bring his force to bear, just might weaken Howe's ability to carry out his plan. Washington ordered a division to cross the Brandywine to attack the left, while his main troops attacked the right. Washington then received intelligence that British troops were not moving as expected and aborted the attack on Knyphausen.

Between noon and one o'clock, Major Joseph Spear of the militia arrived at Sullivan's headquarters and reported that he had just returned from a morning reconnaissance along the Great Valley Road without detecting any sign of the British. The major was, indeed, "confident they are not in that Quarter." How Spear had managed to miss any sign of Howe's column, marching along this very route, was never determined.

Sullivan was suspicious of the report and hesitated before sending it along to Washington, understanding it might mean an end to the attack on Knyphausen. If, however, Howe's move up the Great Valley Road was only a feint followed by a march back to Chadds Ford, Washington's planned attack across the creek might well end in disaster. Sullivan sent the report and Washington called off the attack.

By this time, the British were closing in on Washington from the rear. He now found himself in a defensive position. In the late afternoon, Howe began an attack on the Americans' position on Birmingham Hill, but American artillery and fierce concentrated small arms fire caused him to halt the attack.

The reprieve was short-lived, and after holding off five British attacks that often resulted in very close "musket to musket" combat, the Americans were forced from the hill.

Now Washington's priority was to reform successfully his scattered and broken divisions and to make a withdrawal of the remainder of his army. The Marquis de Lafayette, who had come to observe the attack and attempted to rally the men around him, received a British musket ball in the leg and had to be carried off the field.

After a few minor battles and the loss of eleven thousand men, either killed, wounded or captured, Washington was able to retreat to Chester. Among those captured was Benjamin Rittenhouse, David's brother. The British, not knowing of Benjamin's involvement in the patriot's flintlock factory, negotiated his quick release.

Upon learning of Washington's defeat at Brandywine, the Congress gave $200,000 to Philadelphia's Council of War to apply to defensive concerns. The Council turned the money over to David.

On September 15, David enrolled in the Fourth Battalion of the Philadelphia militia, even though he had been excused from military service. He was then able to arrange for removal of American military supplies from French Creek to Bethlehem. He oversaw the transfer of tons of gunpowder, cartridges, sulfur, and other provisions, including whiskey, to various buildings in Bethlehem.

He was also instructed by the Assembly to set up all the needed wagons for transferring the Treasury and its records to somewhere secure. By the time Howe and his troops entered the city, Congress and the Council of war had removed both seats of the government to Lancaster.

Three weeks later, David, along with all of the members of the Supreme Executive Council, and eight other citizens were appointed to a new Council of Safety. The New Council of Safety was an emergency body that had emergency powers. It had the power to seize provisions and other items necessary to the military. It could also set prices and order sales. The

Council met on a daily basis during the fall and dealt with such problems as treason and other military related issues.

At the same time, David was deeply involved with matters of the Treasury by the Supreme Executive Council that resolved most of its problems by giving orders to David to pay for various matters. David's life would be made a little easier when the Council of Safety abolished on December 6.

On September 16, Washington was able to regroup his troops once he moved then away from the British forces. Now, needing to protect both Philadelphia and Reading, which was a major supply city, he tried to place his troops in a position to protect both.

Howe remained encamped on the Brandywine battlefield for four days instead of following up on his victory and engaging Washington in a decisive war-ending battle. But when Howe learned that the Americans were 10 miles to his north, he sent his army to meet them.

Washington learned of Howe's plans and readied his army for another battle. On September 16, the two armies stood on opposite sides of a valley ready to reprise the Battle of Brandywine. All of a sudden a torrential downpour burst from the skies. The showdown, known as The Battle of the Clouds, became the battle that was never fought.

Following the Battle of the Clouds, Washington moved most of the American army to the Reading Furnace installation to replenish their depleted ammunition supply. Brigadier General Anthony Wayne was left behind with a regiment of troops to harass the rear of the main body of the British Army.

The British, in the preparation for crossing the Schuylkill River so they could attack Philadelphia, were camped at Tredyffrin. When Howe received word that Wayne was planning to ambush him, Howe changed his plans. He decided he would surprise Wayne at his camp in Paoli.

Shortly after midnight on September 21, the British unleashed a shockingly disturbing strike on Wayne and his unprepared regiment. The

British soldiers had been ordered to remove the flints from their rifles and attack with bayonets only. The patriots considered bayonets barbaric. Americans were stabbed or burned when they tried to surrender.

The fifty-three rebels who were killed, and the hundreds of wounded became martyrs. The rest of the war was fought by British soldiers in fear that Wayne's troops would try to avenge the atrocities of the Paoli Massacre.

After the Paoli Massacre, Howe moved his army to Valley Forge. Now, Washington had to make a choice. Should he protect Philadelphia or Reading, the site of his supply base? He knew he could not protect both. Washington chose to protect Reading which afforded Howe an open path to Philadelphia.

With Philadelphia in [the] immediate danger of being invaded by the British, chaos gripped the city. Some people were afraid that the British would burn and plunder everything in sight. Tories were prepared to welcome the British Army warmly. Many patriots closed their businesses and moved out. As a safety measure, the Liberty Bell was moved to Allentown for safe keeping.

On September 26, Lord Cornwallis led a parade of British troops and artillery into Philadelphia. Those sympathetic to England met Cornwallis with jubilation, unaware that the future held nothing but misery in the way of inexorably high food prices and even homelessness.

Even though the capital of the rebels were now in the hands of the British, General Washington, having seen the courage and steadfastness of his troops at Brandywine, was confident enough to plan a major offensive. Howe had posted the bulk of the British Army at Germantown, a village about 5 miles outside Philadelphia. He thought it would be a safe spot from which he could keep an eye on Washington. He was wrong.

When Washington learned that Howe had split his army, he decided to attack Germantown on October 4. Washington was going to use four different units that would simultaneously move into position under cover nightfall. At daybreak, all were to meet a little distance from General

Howe's headquarters. This time, it was the rebels who were going to use the element of surprise.

As the battle commenced into the morning, the patriots had the British retreating. Unfortunately, the fighting took place in dense fog and thick smoke from artillery fire, causing one of the four columns to lose its bearings and causing the other columns to be able to coordinate effectively their efforts.

The British had accumulated a large force at a Germantown mansion named Cliveden, where they had taken refuge. The patriot's artillery bombarded the house, but fearing that Anthony Wayne's men, who were still incensed over the Paoli Massacre, would kill them anyway, British troops refused to come out.

With the British remaining troops in pursuit, Washington's troops retreated to Whitemarsh in disarray. Even though the battle was a defeat for the Americans, it functioned as a boost to morale and self-confidence.

They believed the defeat was the result of bad weather, not poor tactics. The casualty count validated the patriots' enthusiasm: 152 Americans dead, 521 wounded, and over 400 captured. The English suffered casualties 537, plus 14 captured.

David, now a member of the military, did not see service in the battle of Brandywine Creek or Germantown. Several of his cousins, and, of course, his brother, did, however. Among his cousins who served were twenty-year-old Jacob Rittenhouse, a descendant of Wilhelm through his son Gerhard, who served as a Teamster and a drummer; his forty-five-year-old cousin, Joseph, and Joseph's forty-seven-year-old brother, William, both descendants of Wilhelm through his son Nicholas.

After the battle, Washington set up camp on land owned by Henry Scheetz and his wife Catherine Rubincam. Catherine was a descendent of Wilhelm through his son Gerhard and was a cousin of David and Benjamin. Both Henry Scheetz and his son Henry Scheetz Jr served as privates in the volunteer militia of Pennsylvania. Henry Sr served under

General Muhlenberg while Henry Junior served Colonel Samuel Atlee's Battalion.

At the time Howe invaded Philadelphia, General Burgoyne

had been advancing from Canada toward New York, expecting Howe to meet him there. Burgoyne had captured Fort Ticonderoga on July 6 and Fort Anne on July 8. After those battles, British casualties were high. Munitions and rations were low, but the Americans were on the run.

The retreating American army made its way to the safety of Fort Edward on July 12. Burgoyne's troops regrouped in Skenesboro where he decided his next move. Burgoyne decided to send his troops overland, while shipping his heavy artillery down Lake George to Fort Edward.

However, Burgoyne's move to Fort Edward was not as easy as he had anticipated. The Americans cut down trees, destroyed bridges, dammed up streams and used scorched-earth tactics to slow the British down. In addition to finding it difficult to obtain rations, these tactics wore on the British troops who had to constantly remove logs, rebuild bridges and un-dam streams. By the time Burgoyne made it to Fort Edward, the patriots had already left.

General Howe had been attempting to communicate with Burgoyne, but his messengers were usually captured and hanged before they could complete their mission. On August 3, Burgoyne learned that Howe was getting ready to capture Philadelphia and that he would have to look elsewhere for support.

Burgoyne, knowing he was low on supplies, acted on information he had received that Castleton was rich in farm animals and horses, which were desperately needed. He sent a regiment toward the New Hampshire Grants on August 9 to requisition supplies, but on August 16, most of those men were lost in the Battle of Bennington. This battle cost the British close to 1,000 men, and any chance they had to garner the supplies they needed.

By September 1777, Burgoyne's 7000 man army was encamped on the east bank of the Hudson. But, he knew he needed to find safe winter quarters. Burgoyne hated retreat, which he would have to do to if he went to Fort Ticonderoga. He, therefore, chose to relocate to Albany. He also decided to cut communications with his northern troops and to cross the Hudson River while he was in a relatively strong position. As a result, he ordered his rear guard to join him. He then had his army cross the river just north of Saratoga between September 13 and 15.

By September 18, his army had reached a location a little north of Saratoga, which was about 4 miles from the patriot's forces which stretched from the river to Bemis Heights. Realizing the Americans position could be flanked, Burgoyne sent a large force to the west of the American line. Benedict Arnold knew that a British attack on the left was likely, and asked General Gates for permission to move his forces out to Freeman's Farm. Gates denied the request, expecting a frontal assault.

He did, however, permit Arnold to send some riflemen and light infantry out to scout the area. The scouts made contact with Burgoyne's right flank, and the two enemy forces battled for control of Freeman's Farm. The British were victorious, but it cost them ten percent of their forces.

After the battle of Freeman's Farm, Burgoyne's men were exhausted. He, therefore, withdrew his plans to attack again the next day and instead decided to wait for some word that he would be getting assistance from General Clinton in New York.

He desperately needed supplies, and reinforcements because of the continued desertions from his army. On the other side, around 2,000 men joined the patriots, bringing the American army to over 15,000 troops.

Burgoyne, on October 7, led a reconnaissance force consisting of 1,700 men to scout the patriots' left flank. When the Americans became aware of the reconnaissance force, Gates sent one of his companies around the British right, and another against Burgoyne's left.

When some of the Americans made contact, a battle ensued. The initial American attack was highly effective, and Burgoyne ordered a retreat, but his orders never reached his troops and during intense fighting, the center of Burgoyne's forces held, but his flanks were exposed. After the arrival of additional American troops, Burgoyne once again ordered his heavily damaged troops to retreat.

General Arnold, in a drunken rage, left the American headquarters to join the battle when he heard the sound of fighting. When he arrived at the battle scene, he immediately assaulted the British position. The right side of the British line was made up of two earthen strongholds that had been erected on Freeman's Farm, which was defended by light infantry.

Arnold's first attack on the redoubt failed. He then, seemingly without fear, rode through the gap between the two redoubts, which was manned by a company of Canadian irregulars. Some of the American forces then attacked the open rear of one of the redoubts.

Arnold's leg was broken when his horse was shot and fell on him, but one of the positions was taken before darkness halted the fighting. Burgoyne lost nearly 900 men while the Americans lost approximately 150 men.

The next day Burgoyne, whose positions had been continuously sniped [that] by the Americans, were ordered to retreat. Fending off American forays in heavy rain, Burgoyne's army took almost two days to reach Saratoga. However, Gates ordered some of his troops to position themselves on the east side of the Hudson to thwart any crossings.

By the morning of October 13, Burgoyne's army was completely surrounded. On October 17, Burgoyne ceremoniously gave his sword to Gates, who then returned it to him as his army of nearly 6000 troops marched out to surrender their arms to the tune of "Yankee Doodle".

As a result, the British withdrew from Ticonderoga and Crown Point in November, and Lake Champlain by early December. However, General Clinton was now raiding along the Hudson. American troops were deployed south to Albany on October 18, while other detachments were sent to the East.

David became the subject of two poems in 1777. The first poem was written by Rev. Jonathan Odell, a strong loyalist, and was published in the *Royal Gazette*, of New York on September 8. The second poem was published in the *Pennsylvania Evening Post on December 2*. Both poems praised David as a philosopher and scientist, but both poems also demeaned him for going into politics, stating it was the end of David's exaltation as a man of renown, and vice-president of rogues and fools.

From December 6 through the 8th, Washington engaged Howe's troops in skirmishes before deciding to spend the winter at Valley Forge. Washington knew Valley Forge was near enough to the British to keep them from going into the western part of Pennsylvania, yet far enough away to thwart off any forays on his campsite. The valley also was defensible and provided trees for the building of housing for his men.

The majority of the men in Washington's army did not have shoes or proper clothing, and what clothing they had was tattered and torn. The Army immediately began building cabins for housing, and by the start of February, they had constructed over eighteen hundred cabins.

The army had sparse supplies of bread and meat. "Fire cakes", made of the bland mixture of flour and water, was often all they had to eat. Their conditions were so bad that Washington was afraid that his men, at least those who did not desert, were going to starve.

Fortunately, Nathanael Greene, who had just been appointed as Quartermaster, was able to find some supplies, but the amount was totally insufficient. Many of the man died of diseases such as dysentery, smallpox, pneumonia and even typhoid. Almost 2,500 men lost their lives during that winter; almost as many as deserted. Some of the enlisted men's wives were able to provide what comfort they could, such as doing laundry and nursing the wounded.

At first, Congress was unable to help, but by February it was able to supply most of what Washington's army needed, which greatly increased the soldiers' morale. However, there was still one thing lacking. Fortunately, a skilled drill master, Baron Frederick von Steuben, arrived in camp from Prussia, and took on the job of molding the Army into skilled soldiers.

On February 10, 1778, Martha Washington arrived at Valley Forge. In addition to greeting soldiers in their cabins, she visited them in the camp infirmary. She organized approximately five hundred women into a sewing circle that darned socks, knitted new items of clothing, and mended torn and worn pants and trousers. It was a horrible winter, but one that molded the army into the best America had ever had.

CHAPTER 5

What Washington didn't know when he opened his camp at Valley Forge, was that the French had been so impressed with the Americans' victory at Saratoga, that they agreed to make formal both the military, and a trade alliance with the thirteen colonies. They signed the pact on February 6, 1778.

While elated by the news of the victory at Saratoga, David had his hands full trying to fill the constant barrage of orders. His complaining of the lack of funds prompted the Assembly to commence using Loan Office money. David received £13,000 on January 6.

The funds were helpful, but not sufficient. He knew he was just going to have to learn to live with the aggravation of not being able to perform his function properly. The situation only served to worsen David's stomach problems further.

While David was elated by the news from France, the problems he had meeting the state of Pennsylvania's monetary obligations dulled his enthusiasm. The rest of the colonies and the Army, however, stayed in a state of exhilaration for months.

The two were still engaging each other in the early months of the year. One of those skirmishes occurred on March 18 in New Jersey, at Quinton Bridge. While on a foraging mission, a force of the Queen's Rangers, led by Captain John Graves Simcoe, and British regulars, led by

British Lieutenant-Colonel Sir Charles Mawhood, had been informed that American militia was nearby also foraging.

And indeed, a 300 man American militia led by Colonel Asher Holmes was foraging near Quinton's Bridge, which spanned the Alloway Creek.

The British, unbeknownst to the Americans, were on the opposite side of the creek from them. In the early morning hours of March 18, the British moved into a position near the bridge. Holmes, knowing that the English forces were in the area had ordered planks removed from the bridge as a defensive measure.

When one of the American officers saw a British force attempting to move to their rear, he replaced the planks and crossed the bridge in pursuit with 200 men, leaving only 100 defenders behind. Soon afterward, the Americans engaged a British force that had been posted behind a rail fence.

While the Americans skirmished with the British at the fence, a contingent of British forces slipped out of a house near the fence, and cut off their rear flank. Cut off from the bridge; the Americans attempted to cross the creek at another location, but became sitting ducks for the British rifleman. In the confusion of the melee, several militiamen were drowned.

By this time, the main British force was in a position to attempt to cross the bridge to the Americans side. However, American militia led by Colonel Elijah had also arrived at the bridge. Using his two cannons to bombard the British position they were forced to stop the crossing. Most of the American casualties that day were from drowning.

After the battle, Mawhood demanded that the American militia surrender and threatened to burn down the town of Salem if they refused. In addition, he threatened to unleash the loyalist militia to do their will against the women and children of the town.

Holmes promised retaliation on civilians loyal to the British if Mawhood followed through on his threats. By this time, the Americans had re-positioned themselves at Hancock Bridge, just 5 miles from Salem. On the night of March 21, Simcoe, and his Queen's Rangers attacked the sleeping Americans at the bridge. Shouting, "spare no one! Give no quarter!" The British killed at least 20 militiamen, some of whom were attempting to surrender.

The Loyalists also raided the home of a fellow loyalist and Quaker, Judge William Hancock, which the Americans were using as a command center. Hancock and his brother were bayoneted in the scrimmage, although both were known to be staunch supporters of the crown and Quaker pacifists. The sortie by the English became known as the massacre at Hancock's Bridge.

By May 6, 1778, the pain and torture the soldiers had felt during the winter melted with the warm sun and drifted into memories with the soft spring breezes. With the new season upon them, the Americans felt as though celebrations were in order, especially after learning of the newly signed alliance with France.

Washington, along with other military leaders, watched as thousands of his troops performed parade drills, and formations accompanied by the firing of muskets and cannons. Shouts of, "Long live France! Long live the friendly powers! Long live the American States!" filled the air.

England, however, was not so pleased with the turn of events. The British feared a French naval blockade with the new alliance, and Washington realized that the British would have to withdrawal from Philadelphia to prevent this from happening. While he knew the withdrawal would be eminent, he just wasn't sure when it would occur.

As a result, he dispatched Lafayette along with 2,100 troops and five cannons to a point halfway between Valley Forge and Philadelphia, called Barren Hill, to observe the British movements.

Lafayette set up camp at Barren Hill on May 18. He positioned the guns along with a brigade of men near a church that was on higher ground. He posted more men at Ridge Road, leading south, and assigned the guarding of the road to the west to the Pennsylvania militia.

It did not take long for the British to discover the Americans lurking nearby. The British dispatched 5,000 men, and 15 guns to Barren Hill on the morning of May 19. The British planned on flanking the Americans, thus cutting off their route of a retreat.

Approximately 2,000 Redcoats positioned themselves on Lafayette's left flank, while others covered his right flank, leaving Lafayette with his back against the Schuylkill River. After getting into position, the British waited to strike until morning.

The men on Ridge Road learned of the attack and sent a small group to engage in delaying the action, thereby allowing them time to notify Lafayette. However, when the British launched their attack, the militia ran from the battle offering little to no resistance. By that time, Lafayette had also learned that the British had maneuvered up Whitemarsh Road.

Lafayette knew of a small trail running along the low ground that would take him and his men out of the path, and out of the sight of the oncoming British forces. Fortunately, the remaining Americans were able to escape with very few casualties.

When their mission to destroy Lafayette's forces failed, the British troops returned to Philadelphia to join in the evacuation of the city, which was completed by June 19. General Sir Henry Clinton, the new commander of the British Army, decided on moving from Philadelphia to Sandy Hook and then take boats to New York City.

Washington, realizing that Clinton was headed for the safety of New York, and wondered what the best approach should be in engaging the British forces. Washington and his men were divided on strategy, and General Charles Lee's argument that with the French their side, eventual victory for the Americans would be had, and therefore, an all-out assault against a superior force was unnecessary.

Washington rebuked these arguments, but later after another meeting with his commanders at Hopewell, New Jersey, on June 23, he reversed himself and decided to go with Lee's strategy of restraint. However the plan Washington devised was still unacceptable to Lee, who refused to command the 4,000 troops to assault Clinton from the rear. Lafayette, therefore, took the command.

Once Washington had increased the assault troops to 5,000 men, Lee decided he wanted in on the action and took over the command. However, in the midst of battle Lee lost control of the fight by sending troops into battle piecemeal rather than using a coordinated effort. His troops began to scatter, many racing back toward the main American army.

When Washington was briefed on what had happened, he rallied Lee's men, and set up a line along a hedgerow where they were able to hold the British off long enough to let American troops move to the West, where they fought back repeated British attacks. Finally, the British retreated and continued their march to New York. Many believed that the outcome of the battle was the result of the training the troops had received from Von Steuben in February.

In celebration of the British withdrawing from Philadelphia, David joined Owen Biddle, John Lukens, and William Smith in an attempt to view a solar eclipse, but the sky was cloudy and dismal in the morning as the eclipse began. It was not until the afternoon hours that the quartet was able to observe the spectacular sight. While it did not have any real scientific significance, David was able once again to enjoy his science.

Thomas Jefferson, in a letter to David said he had also tried to observe the eclipse, but had no success. According to Jefferson, one of his problems was that he had not yet received the clock David had promised to build for him, and therefore was not able to establish accurate times.

Jefferson, expressing his frustrations with the bickering of partisan politics wrote to David that he was convinced that David was wasting his talents by being involved with government. In urging him to return to science, Jefferson wrote *"there was an order of geniuses above that obligation, and, therefore, exempted from it. No body can conceive that nature ever intended to throw away a Newton upon the occasions of the crown…. Are those powers then, which being intended for the condition of the world, like air and light, the world's common property, to be taken from their proper pursuit to do the commonplace drudgery of governing a single state, a work which may be executed by men of an ordinary stature such as are always and every where to be found?"*

By July 2, the Continental Congress had returned to Philadelphia as well and granted Pennsylvania the sum of $100,000 for the purchase of clothing for the troops. It fell upon David to make the three-day round trip to York to retrieve the funds. Once again, the funds proved helpful but insufficient, certainly to cover any costs of running the state's affairs.

David was continuously scrambling to find resources to enable the state to meet its obligations. There was a continuous shortage of food, ammunition, and men. It was up to the Executive Council to somehow provide funds when food for the Army became critical, but it was barely able to meet the rations necessary.

Even with his other obligations, and problems, and the letter from Jefferson, David remained active as an enlisted man in the Philadelphia militia in Captain Christian Schaffer's company, which was under the command of his friend Colonel John Bayard.

State politics became intense and bitter, mostly due to the problems the Treasury had fulfilling its duty. Despite the trouble facing the state, it was apparent that David's Whig Party, now known as the Constitutional Party, was still in control when in the November elections it won resounding support.

In the meantime, the war continued to be fought. In July, French Vice Admiral Charles Hector, Comte d'Estaing, with a fleet of twelve ships, and 4,000 troops, positioned his ships just outside of the New York harbor. He then established communications with Washington, who had set up his headquarters at White Plains.

Believing his armada would be impeded by the bar leading into the harbor, d'Estaing consulted with Washington, and it was decided that they would attack the British stronghold at Newport, Rhode Island, which had been occupied by the English since 1776.

While part of the Army was still under the command of General John Sullivan, along with the 1st Rhode Island Regiment under the command of Nathaniel Greene, they were to accost the British positions on Butts Hill. The 1st Rhode Island Regiment was comprised of African-Americans, Native Americans, and had a handful of colonists all intermingled.

The French troops would go ashore on Conanicut Island, then crossover to Aquidneck Island, and would combine with the American force at Butts Hill. From there, they would advance against Newport. However, the English anticipated the attack and withdrew from Butts Hill. The Americans occupied the hill with no opposition.

French Marines began disembarking on August 8 to aid in the assault on Newport. But, as they were going ashore, eight British ships could be seen off Point Judith, so d'Estaing, knowing he was outnumbered, commanded his Marines to re-embark. He then turned his ships to do battle with the English. However, the weather turned suddenly dreadful, and the ships were badly scattered or damaged. This forced d'Estaing to quit the battle, and in spite of protests from American commanders, took his ships to Boston for repairs. Without French support, an advancement on Newport was impossible.

Washington notified Sullivan on August 24, that the British planned to send reinforcements to Newport, thereby destroying any prospect of a prolonged siege by the Americans. Sullivan, hoping to cut British troops off, moved his troops to the northern end of the island on Butts Hill. From there Sullivan could see across the valley to Turkey Hill, and Quaker Hill, on which he had placed a couple of units. The units were able to overlook the East Road and the West Road, which led North and South to Newport.

A force, led by British Major General Francis Smith, attacked the American's frontal position on Butts Hill while Hessian forces flanked their rear. The Patriots began to retreat to their main lines. As the British pushed forward, American artillery forced them into retreat. Smith, realizing the British were falling back decided against pursuing them even further.

In the meantime, a column led by British General Friedrich Wilhelm von Lossberg, attacked the American troops in front of Turkey Hill. Slowly pushing them back, the Hessians began to gain the high ground. Though reinforced, the Patriots were finally forced to move back across the valley, and passed through Greene's lines on the American right.

Three British ships then began bombarding the American lines. Green re-positioned his artillery, and with assistance from American batteries on Bristol Neck, forced the ships to abandon their attack. Undaunted, von Lossberg launched an attack on Greene's 1st Rhode Island Regiment, which was able to repel the initial assault but was finally forced to withdraw.

Re-gathering his troops, Green commenced a series of counterattacks and gained some ground back. The Hessians then moved themselves to the top of Turkey Hill. During the night of August 30, the Patriots left Aquidneck Island and sought safety, and encamped at Tiverton and Bristol.

Meanwhile, life went on for the Rittenhouse family as well other families who had to deal with the miseries of the war. John, the grandson of Nicholas, who was living in Roxborough Township, and his wife Margaret Conrad, had a baby girl, Anna Nancy, on September 13.

The final battle of 1778 was fought in Savannah, Georgia, when a British expeditionary force, led by Brigadier General Augustine Prevost, and Lieutenant Colonel Archibald Campbell, began marching toward Savanna. As they approached the city, American forces valiantly tried to fight them off, but were overwhelmed by the superior number of British troops. On December 29, the British were able to take control of Savannah, and establish outposts to recruit loyalists to fight and spy for them.

As 1778 turned into 1779, the colonies, almost without exception, were faced with depreciating money, rising prices, and a shortage of food. Most of these problems existed because of the lack of organized, and controllable patterns of trade, insufficient tax income, and the effects of the war.

However, most people, including the legislative bodies, assumed the causes were actually due to a lack of good public qualities, and heavy corruption. Many citizens believed that it was caused by the greed of individual merchants who seem to be growing richer, while everyone else grew poorer.

One bright note, for both the Pennsylvania State government, and the Federal government, was their stability. While neither one of the governments were able to solve many of their financial problems, they had maintained a sense of steadiness for the last couple of years. This, in turn, began to stimulate other aspects of society, especially the intellectual ones.

For David, happier times would soon arise when his nephew, William Barton, returned from England. When the war first erupted, he had been sent to England to study law. While there, he developed a keen interest in heraldry, and before his return to the states, he had become a master of blazonry.

Young William, unlike his father, Thomas Barton, was very sympathetic to the patriots. His father had become an outspoken critic of the war. So much so, that he had fled to the safety of New York, which the British still controlled. One thing they did have in common though, was his love and admiration for David. As a result, William decided to settle in Philadelphia where, after his admission to the bar, he opened his law practice.

On March 5, David, and a few of his colleagues, called for a meeting at the College of Philadelphia. Concerned about the current lull of the American Philosophical Society, which had been relatively inactive since 1776, David was upset at the lack of meetings and lack of notoriety for the Society. The only mention of the Society in the newspapers, had to do with other groups holding meetings in its facilities. The meeting called by David, and his peers, stirred the slumbering group back into activity.

By March 20, the Society elected new officers; most of them were elected due to their avid involvement in the war against England. Ben Franklin continued as its president, while David, who had served as the Society's secretary, curator, and librarian was elected as vice president. The other vice presidents were William Shipman, Director of the Continental Medical Service, and Thomas Bond.

Then David, and subsequently his estate, became involved in a controversy concerning ownership of a captured ship and its cargo. Gideon Olmstead, and three other fishermen from Connecticut, were captured by the British and forced to do duty on the British ship the *Active*. Eventually, Olmstead and the others successfully mutinied and captured the captain. They then sailed the ship for Egg Harbor, in Pennsylvania waters. Before reaching the harbor, the *Active* was captured by the *Convention*, a warship ship owned by the state of Pennsylvania, and a privateer, the *Gerhard*, which escorted them into port, where it was claimed as a prize for the Connecticut fishermen.

The state of Pennsylvania disputed their claim. Eventually, a state court awarded one-quarter of the value of the prize to the fisherman, another quarter to each of the American ships, and one-quarter to the State. That decision did not set well with Olmstead, and the other fishermen, who took the matter to the Continental Congress.

On May 1, 1779, a judge of the Admiralty Court, George Ross, gave to David, acting as state treasurer, Loan Office certificates in the approximate amount of £11,500, which represented the State's share of the award. David, in turn, posted a bond of £22,000 which was to remain in force until the dispute could be settled. He put the funds he received from Ross into interest-bearing accounts, the income of which was deposited on a regular basis by David.

Congress, sitting as an Admiralty Court, reversed the decision of the Pennsylvania court and awarded the whole prize to Olmstead, and the other fishermen. The Pennsylvania legislature refused to honor the Admiralty Court's decision, especially after it found out that Benedict Arnold, the military governor of Philadelphia since 1778, had purchased a share in Olmstead's claim, and used his influence in Congress to make sure the claim was upheld. Little did David know that the matter would not be resolved until after his demise.

In addition, little did Congress know, that Benedict Arnold was about to become America's most notorious traitor. On May 10, Arnold began negotiating with Sir Henry Clinton, the British commander in New York.

By May 23, in an effort to show sincerity, Arnold give Clinton information regarding the movement of Washington's army.

Shortly after he became involved in the Olmstead matter, David was appointed, on May 25, along with others, to investigate the situation concerning a cargo ship, the *"Victorious"*. It seemed the cargo on the ship was thought to belong to Silas Deane. The Constitutionalists, who thought him guilty of treason, loathed Deane.

It was also believed that Robert Morris conspired with Deane to monopolize the cargo, hold it for a period of time, and then sell it at a highly inflated price. At first, Morris declined to meet with the committee, which had set up a meeting with him at the City Tavern, saying a malady prohibited him from doing so. Thomas Paine was infuriated.

"I saw him yesterday, and he had no such malady," Payne complained to the committee.

"I believe it is important to resolve this issue as quickly as possible," David replied, trying not to get angry himself. "Therefore, I suggest if he will not come to us that we go to him, and do so on the morrow." The other members agreed with David and called upon Morris the next day at his home.

Morris was quite upset over the intrusion, saying the investigation was an effort to besmirch his innocence and integrity, however, after much cajoling, he did agree to answer their questions and even promised a full statement in writing.

The investigation proved that a third-party, associated with Morris, obtained from Deane, the right of first refusal on the cargo. Morris then became involved in a scheme to offer part of the goods to Congress at a reduced price. However, he had to increase the price to Congress when it turned out it violated his contract with the consignment holder. The contract had been written in French, which Morris could not read.

While technically Morris was innocent, David was visibly upset by the fact that the business community viewed such transactions as fundamental to their economic freedom. David, on the other hand, deeply felt that business transactions should be based on morality and patriotism.

Members of the militia started demanding some sort of action regarding the financial problems of the State, and threatened to take matters into their own hands if a satisfactory solution was not found. However, it seemed their support for a solution was one-sided, and close-minded.

When General John Cadwallader, leader of the Philadelphia militia began to speak at a huge town meeting held on July 27, a group of men armed with clubs marched into the meeting with fife and drum playing. They prevented the General from speaking because they did not like his conservative viewpoint.

Acting on the information Benedict Arnold had supplied to him, Clinton began offensive movements on the Hudson River on June 1. Clinton was able to capture Verplanck's Point, and the partially completed garrison at Stony Point, New York. Shortly afterward, the British would begin fortifying the fort.

Later in June, Spain commenced joint naval operations with the French against the English. While they refused to recognize, or enter into an alliance with the Americans, Spain greatly assisted the American cause.

From his position on Buckberg Mountain, Washington was able to observe the British activities. Realizing that the fortification poses a threat to West Point, just twelve miles up the Hudson River, Washington ordered General Anthony Wayne and an elite commando force to attack the fort on July 16. Wayne, with a force of 1200 soldiers, captured the fort after a fierce fight, then destroyed it, and evacuated the area, earning the name "Mad Anthony".

Amidst all of the financial crises he faced with the governing bodies, the political intrigues, and the war raging around him, David was still expected to participate in the useful application of the sciences he so well commanded.

August of that year, he found him once again involved in the Virginia boundary dispute. This time, he was asked to participate in formulating an agreement which would resolve the matter of the boundary between Pennsylvania and Virginia once and for all. By the end of August, all parties to the dispute were in agreement, some more reluctantly than others. The Pennsylvania Assembly quickly approved the agreement when David presented it to them on November 19. However, Virginia did not accept the agreement until December 1, 1780.

On September 2, 1779, Benjamin's third child, daughter Mary, was born in Philadelphia. The next day the siege of Savannah by Continental, and French forces began. After their first defeat at Savannah in December 1778, General Benjamin Lincoln was able to rebuild the American forces to approximately 7000 men.

On September 12, the French naval commander, Admiral d'Estaing began landing troops just below the city of Savannah. The troops included more than 500 recruits from the french colony of Saint Domingue, most of which were Negros, and many of those were former slaves.

On October 3, d'Estaing began a bombardment of the British fortification as well as the city of Savannah. The British fortification remained relatively untouched, but the city was destroyed. The bombardment continued until October 8.

The next morning d'Estaing launched an ill-advised ground attack. The American and allied forces were quickly annihilated to almost the last man. The slaughter lasted for an hour before d'Estaing ordered a retreat. However, it was October 17 before Lincoln and d'Estaing called off the siege.

It was towards the end of that month that a bright meteor graced the southwestern evening sky. Its descent was almost vertical and left behind a slowly dissipating silver trail. After receiving information on its appearance and position from John Page, who had observed it in Williamsburg, David was able to estimate its altitude at the apex and the point of its descent.

He concluded that meteorites were *"… Bodies altogether foreign to the Earth, but meeting with it, in its Annual Orbit, are attracted by it, and entering our Atmosphere take fire and are exploded, something in the manner Steel filings are, when passing thro' the flame of a Candle."* This was an exclamation expounded by a few others, but certainly wasn't accepted by the majority of the scientific community.

Toward the end 1779, David and his fellow Constitutionalists convinced the Assembly that the Provost and Board of Trustees of the College of Philadelphia were Tory sympathizers, and that the colonial charter of the college should be changed to a state university.

The present Board of Trustees and faculty were promptly relieved of their responsibilities, and a new board and faculty were elected. The College of Philadelphia then became the University of the State of Pennsylvania. David was elected to one of the 24 seats on the board and immediately assigned to a position on two of the boards committees.

Tragedy strikes even the noblest of us. While David and Benjamin had lost their mother in 1777, on November 27, they also lost their father, Matthias. Even though his father did not understand or appreciate David's intellect, or talents as a child growing up, the two had become very close over the years. On occasion, such as the observation of the transit of Venus, Mathias even assisted in David's scientific adventures. His father's passing was one more pain that David had to endure.

In December, David's sadness over the loss of his father was eased by his election by the new Board of Trustees as Professor of Astronomy. The board also decided that David should be one of two professors giving instruction in the field of mathematics and natural philosophy. David was excited. He now had the opportunity to teach his favorite subjects to advanced students, and to help initiate a new field of study to students.

The winter of 1779 was by far the coldest that had been experienced in many years. To determine just how cold it was, David and William Smith had a digger probe the frozen tundra. David determined that the frost line was seven and one-half inches deep. The ice layer was anywhere between 16" and 18" thick, and cattle were found frost bitten.

About that time, George Washington decided to set up winter camp at Morristown, New Jersey, again. The compounded problem of the extremely cold winter, and a breakdown of the army's supply system, meant problems for the Continental Army. Once again, Washington had to deal with preventing desertions, and several attempts at mutiny.

CHAPTER 6

At the urging of George Washington, and in an effort to avoid the sort of confusion that enveloped the Olmsted case, Congress established the Court of Appeals in cases of capture. It was to be an appellate court that would hear appeals from state court prize cases, such as the Olmsted case.

In February 1780, David became Vice-Provost of the University, but the curriculum he was to teach there never developed. Disappointed that his opportunity to re-enter academic sciences did not come to fruition, David tried to begin a correspondence with Benjamin Franklin in Paris. However, neither one of the two letters he sent made it into Franklin's hands.

On March 1, the Pennsylvania legislature passed "An Act for the Gradual Abolition of Slavery". It was the first attempt by a state to get rid of slavery in the Western Hemisphere. David and Benjamin Franklin had hoped for more, but in their hearts, they knew that this was a giant step forward in the battle against African slavery. For now, they just hoped that other colonies would follow Pennsylvania's lead.

Then David's attention was drawn away from his problems at the Treasury when he learned that his close friend, Admiralty Judge Francis Hopkinson, was involved in a scandalous proceeding calling for his impeachment and trial on bribery and other charges. To David's relief, Hopkinson was eventually cleared of all wrong-doing in December 1780.

In writing to Benjamin Franklin about his ordeal, Hopkinson expressed his belief that the strength and support he received from David helped him make it through the trial. He told Franklin that his conversations with David were his "chief pleasure",

but he wished they could have been more frequent than they were.

Any relief David may have felt from the tension of his friend's trial and impeachment proceedings were short-lived when he learned that his cousin, Gerhard **[Peter, Gerhard, Wilhelm]** had died in Cresheim, near Germantown. In many ways, David had grown away from his relatives, but he still had a warm spot for many of them, especially his cousins. He wrote a note of condolence to Gerhard's wife, Mary, and her six children.

David's aggravation with his position as State Treasurer, and the misery it caused him, continued. It seemed that David was constantly torn between lack of income, and the demands of the Safety Council. Finally, on April 28, the volcano churning inside him erupted. In an un-David-like moment, he exploded to President Joseph Reed, voicing his anger at the constant passing of revenue requests, when they knew that David was unable to fund their requests.

On May 25, David's world was once again covered with the dark veil of death, when his best friend and protagonist, his brother-in-law, Thomas Barton, passed away in New York.

On June 11, just as David and Benjamin Franklin had hoped, the State of Massachusetts drafted a new Constitution, which included the phrase that "all men are born equal," including black slaves.

August 1780 was not a good month for the Americans. In addition to the defeat suffered by General Gates, another major event occurred. Having the command of West Point, Benedict Arnold, who had been giving General Clinton information on Washington's troops, contacted General Clinton again, but this time commenced making plans to hand over the fort and his men to the British.

On September 21, Arnold met with Major John Andre to make final arrangements to carry out his plan. The plan, however, was discovered before it could be executed, and Andre was arrested. Arnold was able to escape, and make it to the British lines. In an unrelated event a few days later, on September 23, David's 2nd cousin, Garrett Rittenhouse married Catherine Sine, in Hunterdon, New Jersey

After the battle at Camden, General Cornwallis believed that loyalists controlled South Carolina. He began moving north toward Charlotte, North Carolina in mid-September. His movements, however, did not go unnoticed by militia companies from North and South Carolina. Thomas Sumter, and his forces stayed back and harassed British and Loyalist as they established outposts in the back country of South Carolina, while other forces, led by Major William R. Davie, stayed close to Cornwallis' main force as Cornwallis moved northward.

Davie's troops reached Charlotte before Cornwallis, and set a trap for the unsuspecting British officer. Mecklenburg County Courthouse stood at the crossroads of Charlotte's two main roads. The courthouse had a stone wall that stood 3.5 feet high, between two of its pillars that was used as the local market. Davie put his militia three rows deep at the north end of the courthouse. One of the rows was behind the stone wall. He also put cavalry companies on the east and west sides of the courthouse, to cut off any retreat, using the roads leading away from the courthouse. There was a house on the southern road that Davies expected the English to use for their approach to Charlotte. He put a company of 20 men behind the house.

As his column approached Charlotte, Cornwallis sent Major George Hanger, second in command to the British Legion, to use caution in investigating the town for the militia. Hanger and his cavalry, however, threw caution to the wind and galloped into town. Troops behind the house opened fire, but could not stop Hanger's advance.

As he approached the courthouse, he was met by heavy fire from the line of militia manning the positions behind the wall. When the first militia line fell back to make way for the second line, Hanger thought they were in retreat, and continued his charge. Caught in a cross-fire from the second line, and the cavalry companies which were stationed to the east and west, Hanger was wounded in the battle. His cavalry scattered in a hasty non-organized retreat. Cornwallis ordered the legion and the main army's light infantry into the fray. Davie, knowing he was outnumbered, quickly withdrew his men.

Cornwallis now realized that the South was not as secure for the British as he had once thought. He had intended on going on to Hillsboro, but because of the illness to of two of his commanders, Cornwallis decided to stay in Charlotte. But, he was constantly harassed by American militia who made it difficult for him to communicate with forces in the countryside.

One of Cornwallis' commanders protecting Cornwallis' left flank was Major Patrick Ferguson of the 71st Foot. When he arrived on the scene in early September, he issued a warning to the militia to surrender or suffer the consequences. Instead of surrendering, six militia commanders, (Isaac Shelby, James Johnston, Benjamin Cleveland, John Sevier, Joseph McDowell and William Campbell), decided to plan an attack on Ferguson.

Ferguson learned of the land attack and decided to retreat to the safety of Lord Cornwallis' army. However, the Patriots caught up with them and surprised the loyalists at Kings Mountain on October 7. They surrounded them and then attacked. The battle lasted for an hour and resulted in heavy casualties for the British, including Ferguson, who was critically shot. Upon seeing their commander fall, his men surrendered.

Some Patriots who were seeking revenge for a massacre of militiamen at the Battle of Waxhaws by Tarleton's men yelled the battle cry "Remember Tarleton's Quarter." They then viciously attacked Ferguson's men, even after their surrender. Finally, the American officers re-established control, and fearful of Cornwallis' advance, they retreated. However, in the end, Cornwallis abandoned his plan of invasion of North Carolina and he, himself, retreated to South Carolina.

On October 26, David's 14-year-old 2nd cousin, Joseph S. Rittenhouse (Lott, William, Gerhard, Wilhelm) married 18-year-old Mary Ann Wright, in Hunterdon, New Jersey. They had their first child, Susannah Elizabeth the following year.

About this time, David began constructing a new observatory for himself, and Philadelphia. The Philosophical Society had an observatory in the State House yard that had dilapidated to the point that it needed a lot of repairs. The Society's first inclination was to repair it and appointed David, Biddle, and Lukens to do just that, but later it decided to demolish the relic.

When Timothy Matlock learned of David's intention of building the new observatory closer to his home, he convinced the Assembly to give aid, and assistance to David's endeavor. The assembly unanimously voted to give David £252 to use for the project, which he constructed later in 1781 on the corner of Seventh and Mulberry streets.

On January 1, 1781, all 11 regiments from the Pennsylvania Line, a total of 1,500 soldiers in all, became involved in mutiny, murder, and intrigue when they insisted that their three-year enlistments had expired. When General Anthony Wayne refused their demands to be released from their commitment, there occurred a debacle. In a drunken rage, they killed three officers and went AWOL from the Continental Army's winter camp at Morristown, New Jersey.

The mutiny delighted British General Henry Clinton, but horrified Pennsylvanians. David realized that the uprising of the soldiers were due in large as the result of the worsening financial crisis that gripped not only the state, but also Congress.

In 1780, Continental currency held steady, that is until the end of the year, when it began to depreciate, and there was little he could have done about it.

British General Clinton's representatives met with the members of the Pennsylvania Line, with offers of a full pardon and payment of the pay due them by the Continental Army if they fought for the English. The mutineers rejected Clinton's offer, and decided to march to Princeton and capture it instead. They succeeded in their endeavor on January 3, and with some of Clinton's men as hostages, they set their sites to march onto Philadelphia, and reach Congress.

However, before commencing their their march, they sent representatives to meet with General Wayne, who had been tailing them. In addition to airing their grievances, they handed over the hostages, who were eventually executed by the Americans.

With their position now strengthened with their show of patriotism, they met with General Wayne and Congressional President Joseph Reed on January 7. Three days later they were able to reach an agreement. Those men who wanted to discharge would be discharged immediately and those men who wished to re-enlist were given furloughs and bonuses. About 750 of the men opted for discharges, while the other 750 took their furloughs and bonuses.

Details of the agreement spread quickly among the military, and led to another mutiny in New Jersey. However, General George Washington was in no mood to tolerate the uprising. He had to act swiftly. He instructed the New England soldiers to arrest and disarm the New Jersey mutineers. Two of the leading mutineers were then executed. David believed that Washington's actions kept the Continental Army from falling apart, even though more Americans were now fighting for the British than against them.

Before David could complete his observatory, he couldn't help thinking about the letter he had received from John Page in October 1779, regarding the sighting of a meteor. Page was the Lieutenant Governor of Virginia at that time, and had served during the war under the Virginia state militia. He had also served as a delegate for the Constitutional Convention in 1776, and this is how he and David befriended one another.

Page had referred in his letter to a little-known force called, "magnetism". Those comments heightened his Interests in the properties of such science.

Magnetism was a mystery, and while there were many theories to account for it, none of them held up under scrutiny and experimentation. David's theory held that iron was comprised of magnetized particles that constantly hold their attractive force, and that each particle had a North and South Pole. He even described experiments that illustrated his concept of magnetic dipoles.

His experiments were soon pushed aside by the continuing news about the war. The now British Brigadier General, Benedict Arnold, led his 1,600 troops, that sailed up the James River at the beginning of January, into Westover, Virginia. They would leave on January 4, 1781, and arrived at the capital city of Richmond the very next afternoon. To his surprise, Richmond was virtually undefended.

Thomas Jefferson, then governor of Virginia, in anticipation of the Arnold's advance, had hastily moved all arms and other military stores of records from the city to a foundry five miles outside Richmond. However, Arnold was approaching the city more quickly than expected. Jefferson then decided to move them to Westham, about eight miles north.

But before he could move the records, Arnold's men attacked and burned the foundry, and marched to Westham. When Arnold realized that Baron Friedrich Wilhelm von Steuben and his men were guarding Westham, he decided to return to Richmond, which was defended by only 200 militiamen. Arnold quickly captured the city and then burned it to the ground.

After British victories in South Carolina, General Nathanael Greene, now the commander of the American Army in the South, decided to divide his troops so he could fight the British on multiple fronts. Three hundred riflemen, and 700 militiamen were placed under the command Brigadier General Daniel Morgan who planned on attacking the British in the hinterland.

Cornwallis was concerned that Morgan may be able to convince Patriots living in the rural areas to join him. He sent Banastre Tarleton, who commanded 1,100 British troops and loyalists, to intercept Morgan. When Morgan realized that Tarleton was chasing him, he decided to stand and fight at a river at Cowpens.

Morgan had ordered his militiamen on the front line to fire two volleys at the attacking British, and then fall back. Thinking the Americans were in a rout, the British kept advancing. Morgan then had his riflemen commence a volley of concentrated rifle fire on the unsuspecting British troops. Then he sent his Calvary into the battle along with the reappearance of the militia. After a bloody battle, Tarleton fled with his demolished army.

Cornwallis, however, continued to chase the Americans through North Carolina. Greene and his forces managed to elude Cornwallis, and make it to Virginia. Cornwallis decided to let his tired troops rest at the Dan River. Once in Virginia, Greene began recruiting forces from the patriotic communities. He knew he would have to once again face Cornwallis' troops, and he wanted to be ready. Once he believed he had a sufficient Army, he returned to North Carolina. On March 14, he camped with his man around Guilford Courthouse.

On March 15, Cornwallis led 1,900 British soldiers against Greene's 4,000 plus regulars and militia. Greene and his men fought the battle for two hours before Greene ordered a retreat. While it was a tactical victory for the English, Cornwallis lost more than 25 percent of his men. Greene's army remained close to full strength. Following the battle at Guilford Courthouse,

General Cornwallis marched his men to Wilmington, North Carolina, and eventually to Yorktown, Virginia.

On March 20, Jacob Rittenhouse (Gerhard, Peter, Gerhard, Wilhelm) married Catherine Maria Salome in Whitehall Pennsylvania, and Susanna Elizabeth Rittenhouse (Joseph S., Lott, William, Gerhard, Wilhelm) was born in Hunterdon, New Jersey.

Around the same time, David's nephew, William Barton, gained notoriety for his treatise "Observations on the Nature and Use of Paper Credit", that he had published earlier in the year. In it, he had proposed the establishment of a national bank. He was awarded an honorary Master of Arts degree from the University of Pennsylvania over his work, and on June 14th, married Elizabeth Rhea.

Elizabeth was the niece of Continental Congressman, Jonathan Bayard Smith. Smith was a successful businessman in Philadelphia. He was also an avid supporter of American Independence, and served with David as a member of the Council of Safety in 1775, and like David, he was one the founders and trustees of the University of the State of Pennsylvania in 1779.

Smith was elected as a delegate to the Continental Congress in 1777, and served in that body until November 1778. He was a signer of the Articles of Confederation for Pennsylvania, as well as a Lieutenant Colonel in the Pennsylvania Militia. In addition to being a Grand Master of the Masons, he was an elected member of the American Philosophical Society.

Alexander Hamilton, after reading Barton's paper, decided to present the idea of a national bank to Robert Morris, Jr. He believed it just might help the struggling country finance the Revolution. He convinced Morris, the Congressional Superintendent of Finance, to introduce a bill to the Continental Congress calling for the establishment. Morris had a long history with Hamilton, as he was one of the signers of the Declaration of Independence, and was known as the "Financier of the Revolution".

In response to the bill, on May 26, 1781, Congress chartered the President, Directors, and the Bank of North America, as a private bank and financial institution. Neither David nor his friend, Thomas Jefferson were particularly enthused about the formation over the bank. They both viewed that the bank would present an opportunity for the wealthy to obtain more wealth, while not giving ample opportunities to the other people in society.

The American forces began a siege of Yorktown, Virginia. Washington, heading a force of 17,000 mixed French troops and Continentals, pitted forces against Cornwallis' 9,000 troops. It turned out to be the most important battle of the Revolution.

Cornwallis had just chosen Yorktown, a village on the Chesapeake, for his headquarters. Unbeknownst to Cornwallis, a French fleet under the command of Admiral François left the French colony of Saint Domingue, which changed it's name to Haiti in 1804, for the Chesapeake Bay at about the same time. Washington realized he could have Cornwallis trapped. Washington knew a British retreat by sea would be blocked by the French fleet. Washington sent Lafayette, along with 5000 American troops, to block an English retreat from Yorktown by land.

Washington had completely encircled Cornwallis and Yorktown by September 28, and used artillery and cannon to bombard the English position constantly. After three weeks of punishment, Cornwallis realized he was defeated and surrendered to Washington in a field at Yorktown on October 17.

The out-manned, out-gunned, and usually, out-maneuvered, Americans had won their war against the most powerful nation on earth. Washington's victory essentially sealed a victory, and independence for the United States.

Cornwallis sent his second in command, Brigadier General Charles O'Hara, to the surrender ceremony on October 19. There, O'Hara presented Washington's second in command, Benjamin Lincoln, with Cornwallis' sword. Cornwallis, who claimed an illness, stated it prevented him from attending.

When David heard of Cornwallis's surrender he, like most Americans, regardless of what their sympathies were, felt relieved that the war had ended. Maybe life could get back to something resembling normal. David, thinking of his cousin, John Gorgas, Jr (Suijten, Nicholas, Wilhelm), knew that he would have been happy as well with the end of the war. Unfortunately, John died on July 1, several months prior, in Germantown. David thought maybe now he would be able to immerse himself in his beloved sciences once again. However, America had other plans for him. But, before those plans could be put in effect, David had to run one more gauntlet of fire which was created by a serious illness.

The political climate was changing. David's friends had lost some support in the state's 1781 election. The Assembly was now split between the Constitutionalists, whom David supported, and the Republican-Democrats. While David had no problem being reelected as the State Treasurer, he sensed a growing political hostility.

David's accounting to the Assembly was due at the end of the year, but in November, after the elections, David reported to them that a serious illness would prevent him from giving his reports until after the first of the year. The assembly gave David the extra time he needed, but the rumors began to fly. Many people thought that David was attempting to cover up some misdeed on his part. He was even accused of misapplication of funds. Fortunately, for David, the rumors began to quickly cease, and by January 1782, the people once again held him in high esteem.

But, political intrigues still swirled around him. Robert Morris, an adversary of David, approached him with the offer of a new Congressional position. According to Morris, he wanted David to act as Congresses' financial overseer of Pennsylvania's treasury. David originally declined the position.

In April, the Pennsylvania Assembly passed a financial reform act that created a new position of Comptroller General with far-reaching authority over the state's finances. The position was to collect taxes, settle accounts due to the state, and settle claims against it. The person holding the title, was empowered to issue subpoenas and writs of attachment, and to put debtors in jail.

One of Robert Morris' business associates, John Nicholson, was appointed to the position. While he had tremendous opportunities to improve the fiscal administration of the state, he also had the power to cause political mischief. However, even after his appointment, Nicholson had little effect on the deepening financial crisis that gripped the state, and on April 5, 1793, the State House of Representatives resolved to impeachment. Nicholson would eventually be acquitted, but resigned all public offices in 1794.

After William Barton's return to American, David found his conversations with his nephew to be particularly therapeutic. As a lad, William often spent many hours with his uncle in his lab. His curious mind and thirst for knowledge were evident even then. Now that he was back from his studies in England, his intellectual capacity delighted David. David was especially captivated by his nephew's knowledge of heraldry.

While he was in England, he was able to visit many of his European relatives on his father's side, as well as on his mother's side, and became well acquainted with his ancestor's coats of arms. Now, back in America, young Barton was becoming well known for his knowledge in heraldry, as well as being an able lawyer. It delighted David to see his young nephew becoming prominent and successful.

In May 1782, shortly after John Adams successfully negotiated a treaty of Amity with the Netherlands, which recognized America as an independent country, Arthur Middleton of South Carolina, Elias Boudinot of New Jersey, and Edward Rutledge of South Carolina called upon Barton, to assist them with the Great Seal of the United States. They knew Barton was well schooled in heraldry, and asked him to assist in the design of the seal. These four men would make up the third committee, as Congress had rejected the two previous committees' designs.

Congress had been searching for a favorable design since the signing of the Declaration of Independence on July 4, 1776. Immediately after the declaration was signed, Congress appointed Ben Franklin, John Adams, and Thomas Jefferson as a committee to design the seal. Theirs was a daunting task because seals usually represented a principality, and would depict the coat of arms of a family or an individual. To design a seal for a republic was a completely different matter. It would be one designed for a republic.

The second committee consisted of James Lovell, John Morin Scott, and William Churchill Houston, who incorporated the help of Francis Hopkinson. Hopkinson had designed the American Flag in 1777, which consisted of thirteen stripes, and stars on a blue field representing American as a new Constellation. The stars were to have said to be in honor David. However, their designs were put on the table as well, until the third committee was appointed in 1782.

Barton's first design, which he described, but did not illustrate, used among other things the constellation of 13 stars in a shield with red and white stripes as well as an olive branch as an emblem of peace, all of which would be placed on the left side. The left side would also depict a maiden with loose auburn tresses falling from a crown radiating gold and a sky-blue fillet filled with silver stars. She wore a long, loose white gown bordered with green. She had a scarf made of stars draped from her right shoulder to her left shoulder. She wore a girdle with the word Virtue across it. Also for the first time in an Eagle was included in the design.

On the right side, he described an American warrior in full military uniform. He also used the motto *"In Vindiciam Libertatis"*. On the reverse side of the seal, he placed a pyramid with 13 steps and an all seeing eye. The 13 steps were a symbolism of the original 13 colonies.

He then redesigned the seal with little changes and submitted the illustration to the committee. The committee, being satisfied with Barton's illustrated design, approved it and submitted it to Congress on May 9, 1782. Congress, however, was not satisfied and on June 13 referred it to Charles Thompson, Secretary of Congress.

Thompson put the Eagle as the central figure of his design specifying that it was an American Eagle and put in its right talons a bundle of arrows instead of the flag that Barton had suggested. Borrowing from the first committee he placed an olive branch in its left talons.

For the crest, he used 13 stars surrounded by clouds as depicted by the second committee. He arranged the red and white stripes, which the second committee depicted, as diagonal and which Barton depicted as horizontal, in chevrons. He then presented the changes to Barton.

Barton changed it by inserting pales for the chevrons and restored his Eagle. He also specified that the number of arrows held in its talons should be thirteen. He gave the design to Thompson then submitted it to Congress as, "Mr. Burtons improvement on the Secretary's device." On June 24, 1782, Congress adopted the device as the Great Seal of the United States.

During that year, loyalists began leaving America and were heading to Nova Scotia, and New Brunswick. Canada was also a favorite destination. Many members of the Rittenhouse family, who had remained uncommitted to the patriotic cause due to their Mennonite beliefs, were among those fleeing to Canada.

Even after Cornwallis' defeat at Yorktown, small skirmishes between British and American troops, such as the skirmish of Combahee Creek on August 27, continued. In Wheeling, West Virginia, Fort Henry was attacked by 40 loyalists and the 250 of their Indian allies.

The final battle of the revolution took place at Fort Henry in Wheeling, West Virginia on September 11, 1782, when approximately 500 Indians and a handful of British soldiers attempted to take the fort. The Patriots were able to prevail because of the heroics of a teenage girl by the name of Betty Zane.

During the two-day siege of the fort, its gunpowder supply had dwindled to a critically small amount. After being informed that there was gunpowder in the Zane family barn, it was decided that someone had to be daring enough to retrieve as much gunpowder as they were able to from the barn. Young Betty volunteered for the duty.

Running to the family's house under fire from both the Indians and the Redcoats, Betty was able to retrieve a tablecloth from the family's house, rush to the barn, fill the tablecloth with gunpowder and make it back to the fort without injury.

In September 1782, John Adams, John Jay and Benjamin Franklin, distrustful of the French political position chose to exclude the French from the peace talks and began officially to negotiate a peace treaty directly with Britain. By November 30, preliminary articles of peace were signed by Britain, and the United States.

When on December 14, the British finally left Charleston, South Carolina, David took a deep sigh, and knew 1783 was definitely looking promising.

CHAPTER 7

The January 18, 1783, meeting of the American Philosophical Society was drawing to a close. "Gentlemen, gentlemen," boomed the chairman's voice over the din of private conversations being held by the members. He waited to continue until the members slowly took their seats. "We have concluded all of the old business on our agenda for today. Is there any new business to be considered?"

Thomas Jefferson rose from his seat. "Mr. Chairman, it is my belief that this August body should respond to the great and everlasting assistance provided to this country by the French monarchy and the French people by bestowing upon them, and their King, a prize worthy of the devotion they demonstrated in the recent war with England."

Several of the other members loudly voiced approval. "And my dear Mr. Jefferson, do you have a specific proposal in mind, or is it your intent that we form a committee to decide how we should honor the French and their monarchy?"

Jefferson continued, "It is my belief that no committee could do more perfect justice to our former brothers in arms than what I am about to propose. We have in our midst, a man of great genius, not only in the sciences, but also a man of great artistic talent. I am of course speaking of our own world-renowned member, Mr. David Rittenhouse. I would, therefore, propose that, should he agree to do so, we enlist Mr. Rittenhouse to make an orrery to present to the King of France, and his people. After all, it is most fitting that we present the people of France with an artifact that is both eloquent and functional."

The hall fell silent as all eyes shifted to David. He rose slowly from his seat. Deep in his heart he knew that physically and emotionally the task was beyond him. The rigors of the war and the financial pressures on him as treasurer of the state of Pennsylvania had reduced him to a state of weariness he had never before encountered. But he knew that the Society would be disappointed if he did not agree to Jefferson's proposal. The Society had always been able to depend on him and he was not about to let it down now.

"Should this esteemed body deem me worthy of accomplishing a tribute sufficient to present to the King of France, it would be my great honor to accept that duty." With that, the meeting concluded as did Jefferson's proposal. The orrery was never made nor was a tribute to the French people forthcoming from the Society. But, David was able to rest his mind that once again he did not let the society down.

Despite the turmoil and political intrigue that David faced daily as a result of his position as state treasurer, he still found time to accommodate the needs of his friends. George Washington was one of those friends.

"Philadelphia, February 7, 1783
Sir--it is with great honor I present to you the spectacles and reading glasses with this letter. I have ground and perfected them to the specifications you communicated to me earlier. They are given in appreciation for the bold leadership and courage you displayed during our war with England. Without your leadership and courage, we would still be struggling under tyranny. I am Sir, your most humble and devoted servant."
D. Rittenhouse

Washington was extremely grateful for his friend's kindness, and responded:

"Newburgh, Feb. 16, 1783

Sir- I have been honored with your letter of the 7th and beg you to accept my sincere thanks for the favor conferred upon me, in the glasses- which are very fine; but more particularly, for the flattering expressions which accompanied the presents.

The spectacles suit my eyes very well- as I am persuaded the reading glasses also will when I get more accustomed to the use of them. At present, I find some difficulty in coming at the proper focus; but when I do obtain it, they magnified perfectly, and show those letters very distinctly, which at first appear like a mess blended together and confused. With great esteem and respect, I am, Sir, your most obedient and humble servant.

Go. Washington

David had made the glasses according to specifications sent to him by Washington, whom he so admired. The respect and admiration the two giants of history shared for one another was reflected in many other ways throughout their lives, and even thereafter. On other occasions, David either repaired or presented Washington with new surveying equipment of his own making. One such piece of equipment was a Vernier compass, often called a Rittenhouse compass since David was the first to make one.

In April of 1783, the Supreme Court of Massachusetts, Chief Justice William Cushing presided in the case of *Commonwealth vs Jennison*. Nathaniel Jennison was a slave owner, and was charged with assault and battery upon Quok Walker in September of 1781. Jennison's defense was that Quok was a run-away slave, however, the state's constitution of 1780, abolished slavery in that state, and made slavery illegal. Jennison was found guilty, and fined forty shillings. Abolitionists throughout the New England states were encouraged by the news of the decision, and by the year 1790, no slaves were recorded on the consensus in that state.

Soon thereafter, the American Philosophical Society reorganized, following closely the organization of the Royal Society. It created a 12-man Council and elected David, Thomas Jefferson, Thomas McKean, Ezra

Stiles, Francis Hopkinson, and John Witherspoon along with six others to serve on the Council. The outspoken Hopkinson led the Society.

He, like David, believed the Society had been absent from scientific endeavors for far too long. He believed if the trend continued, the American scientific community would be held in contempt by the rest of the world. Also like David, he believed that nature was an open book, but that proper methods should be used to investigate its phenomena.

The University faculty, which comprised the largest number of members, however, disagreed with his position. They felt that science contended more upon learning, rather than upon the right methodology of unlocking it secrets. When David revealed that he believed the same as Hopkinson, the faculty begrudgingly accepted Hopkinson's ideas.

One of Hopkinson's persuasion was the resurrection of an idea suggested by David before the war. Hopkinson was determined to build a hall for the Society, and he, in fact, turned over to the Society a vacant piece of land that he owned, along with its mortgage. The other portion of land, was granted by the state of Pennsylvania. The lots were across the street from David's home, and next to the lot on which he was building his observatory.

David, Samual Vaughan, the architect for the new Philosophical Hall, and Hopkinson were appointed to plan the erection of the building. However, after consulting with the Library Company of Philadelphia, they were persuaded to collaborate with the Library Company in its effort to obtain matching lots on the east and west sides of State House Square. One lot would be used by the Society, and the other by the Library Company.

This plan presented both a problem, and an opportunity for David. If they proceeded in concert with the Library Company, then the Hopkinson lot would lay dormant while accumulating taxes and mortgage interest. To offset these charges, David decided to rent it from the Society. As a temporary solution, the Society requested that David keep its hundred and fifty volume library in his home.

On July 23, 1783, Benjamin Harrison, then Governor of Virginia, decided that while the war was in a lull, and with no treaty with England yet, it was time to move forward between distinguishing the line between Virginia and Pennsylvania. Plan after plan for defining that boundary under the agreement of 1779 was introduced, but the war interfered with the progression of any of them.

To this, he dispatched a letter to John Dickenson, president of the Pennsylvania Supreme Executive Council, expressing his belief in the urgency of completing the surveying necessary to determine the boundary line.

The letter prompted him to seek out David at his home.

"My dear David, I know you have been overburdened for lo these many years as state treasurer, and I might add, as the country's most eminent scientist. This state must once again call upon your services," Dickenson said, as he paced the parlor in David's home.

David was standing next to his fireplace underneath a picture of his sister Esther, who died in 1774. "It is true. I am weary, especially of the treasurership. However, as you are aware, I have never shied away from duty when called upon by the state, though I must confess that at times I do find solace in my sciences."

"It is your sciences that I must ask you to employ for the state of Pennsylvania," Dickenson said as he sat on David's sofa. He seemed more at ease than he had been since arriving at David's house.

"I'm already commissioned for three unfulfilled surveys. Am I to assume that you wish to add a fourth to that list?" he queried, as he gently swirled his aperitif in its glass.

"You are correct, my good sir," Dickenson said as he stood and accepted a glass of sherry from David's long time free-black maid. "However, this one is not to be added to a list. It is to be completed forthwith."

"What is the urgency, if I may be so rude to ask?"

"I have received a letter from Benjamin Harrison, the Governor of Virginia. He brought up, once again, the completion of the distinction of the boundary between our state and his, which should have been completed in 1779."

David was well aware of the agreement he helped forge between the two states to have the disputed boundary line established back in 1779. "You wish me to serve on a commission to now resolve the boundary difference between our states?"

"That is correct, my good friend," Dickenson said as he sat himself back down on the sofa. "I would like you to hand-pick three others to represent Pennsylvania. Harrison has already pointed the Reverend James Madison, John Page, Robert Andrews, and the renown surveyor Andrew Ellicott."

"All good men, all good men indeed," David said as he sat in one of the parlor chairs. "I would propose, in return, you appoint John Ewing, Thomas Hutchins, John Lukens. I assume you wish me to be one of our delegates."

David then began the task of gathering up the equipment the Pennsylvania team would need to complete their portion survey and supply the planned observatory which would allow an extension of the Mason-Dixon line westward.

For the Virginians, life was not so simple. They had made plans for borrowing some of the instruments they would need from the College of William and Mary. They also made arrangements to import needed astronomical tables from Europe. Unfortunately, severe winter storms delayed their importations.

During the second week of September, 1783, David had been appointed along with Thomas Hutchins, and Nathan Sellers, to see if it was feasible to establish a waterway between the Susquehanna River and the Schuylkill River.

Their mission was: "to view the different roads leading from the Susquehanna to Reading and Philadelphia, and to point out the most practical mode of improving the same; also to consider the most probable way of opening a communication between the rivers Susquehanna and Schuylkill-to form an estimate to the expense of carrying the above designs into execution and to report their proceedings with all possible execution to the next House of Assembly." Also "to receive the proposals of such person or persons as may offer lands to the public for the purpose of building a town or towns on the east bank of the Susquehanna."

With his co-appointees, David knew he was among some of the finest surveyors.

Thomas Hutchins was born in New Jersey in 1730, and was given the rank of ensign with the British Army when he was only 16 years old. In 1772, he became a member of the American Philosophical Society. During the Revolutionary War, he became a sympathizer to the American cause, and in 1780 resigned from his position with the British Army. However, an investigation was led into his activities during the war, as a secret mailing address, and coded letters became unearthed, and in 1780 France held him on grounds of treason. He was able to flee France with the assistance of Benjamin Franklin, where he returned to the states. In 1781, he was appointed the first and only Geographer of the United States.

Nathan Sellers had served in the Revolutionary War, and fought at Brandywine, and Germantown. He was commissioned by the Safety Council of Pennsylvania in 1777 to make survey of the Delaware River just prior to General Howe's advancement on Philadelphia. However, due to his expertise with wire-working, he was pulled from the war by an Act of Congress. He would go on to use his skill for the advancement of the cause, which was crucial to paper making and cartridge making, and which had both been embargoed by the British during the war.

The peace negotiations with England that had begun in April of the previous year, were consummated with the signing of the Treaty of Paris on September 3, 1783. The United States negotiators were John Jay, Henry Laurens, John Adams, and Benjamin Franklin. France, Spain, and the Netherlands forged their own separate agreements with the British.

The preamble to the agreement stated the treaty to be "in the name of the most holy and undivided Trinity", and declares the intention of both parties to "forget all past misunderstandings and differences" and "secure to both perpetual peace and harmony". The treaty acknowledged the sovereignty of the United States as well as establishing boundaries between the United States and Canada.

The United States would own all of the area east of the Mississippi River, north of Florida, and south of Canada. Fishing rights off Canadian coasts would be granted to the United States. America agreed to allow British merchants and Loyalists to use judicious means to recover their property. It seemed to many that the United States gained more than the British through the treaty. However, the view of the British was that if the United States was treated favorably it would become a highly profitable trading partner with Britain.

It was also agreed that each side's prisoners of war would be released and that any property belonging to the English army found in the United States is to become the property of the United States. This clause included slaves. It was also decided that each country should be given continuous access to the Mississippi River.

And on November 25, 1783 – the last of the British troops pulled out of New York city.

George Washington had been contemplating where he wanted to direct his life now that the war was over. He longed to return to Mount Vernon and resume his farming, and to be with his family. He knew what he had to do.

On December 19, 1783, a large white horse with a rider dressed in full officer's uniform majestically made its way through the streets of Annapolis, Maryland. Large crowds gathered around the horse and its rider, cheering and shouting as the horse slowly made its way through the crowd to the Maryland Statehouse. The rider slowly dismounted, as a servant took control of the horse's reins. Dusting himself off as he stretched his body to its full height of six foot four inches, he slowly made his way into the Maryland Statehouse as the crowd clamored about him. Suddenly a man emerged from the door yelling at the crowd to get back.

An exhausted General Washington turned and waved to the crowd. He had spent the last four days preparing for this day.

Washington addressed his intentions to congress the following day about his desire to retire from the military, and was looking for direction as to whether it would be more appropriate to do so with a formal letter, or in front of a public audience. It was determined that a public audience would be the most suited, and on December 22, a feast was held in his honor at Mann's Tavern.

Washington's formal resignation would take place on December 23, and in his speech, he spoke these words:

> "Happy in the confirmation of our independence and sovereignty, and pleased with the opportunity afforded the United States of becoming a respectable nation, I resign with satisfaction the appointment I accepted with diffidence; a diffidence in my abilities to accomplish so arduous a task; which however was superseded by a confidence in the rectitude of our cause, the support of the supreme power of the Union, and the patronage of Heaven."

Washington's willingness to return to civilian life was an essential element in the transformation of the War for Independence into a true revolution. During the war, Congress had granted Washington powers equivalent to those of a dictator and he could have easily taken solitary control of the new nation. Indeed, some political factions wanted Washington to become the new nation's king. His modesty in declining the offer and resigning his military post at the end of the war fortified the republican foundations of the new nation.

Although he asked nothing for himself, Washington did enter a plea on behalf of his officers: "...I should do injustice to my own feelings not to acknowledge, in this place, the peculiar services and distinguished merits of the gentlemen who have been attached to my person during the war. It was impossible the choice of confidential officers to compose my family should have been more fortunate. Permit me, sir, to recommend in particular, those who have continued in the service to the present moment, as worthy of the favorable notice and patronage of Congress."

The patronage Washington requested seemed most pressing, as the army had narrowly survived several mutinies and a near-attempted coup the previous autumn. The veteran officers who had helped to keep the army intact desired western lands in acknowledgment for their service. Their claims would constitute a major issue for the new American government as it attempted to organize the settlement of what had been the colonial back-country.

Washington concluded: "Having now finished the work assigned to me, I retire from the great theatre of action; and bidding an affectionate farewell to this August body, under whose orders I have so long acted, I here offer my commission, and take any leave of all the employments of public life."

General Washington's respite proved extremely brief. He was unanimously elected to the first of two terms as President of the United States in 1788.

The Treaty of Paris was ratified on January 14, 1784, by the Confederation Congress. The ratification officially brought the American Revolution to its victorious finalization. Ratified copies were then sent back to Europe for confirmation by the other signatories. France legalized the treaty in March 1784. British agreement took place in April. The ratified versions were exchanged in Paris on May 12, 1784. While the treaty ended hostilities, both resentments and suspicions remained. Tensions between England and the United States would erupt twenty-eight years later in the War of 1812.

By April 1784, the expedition to map the Pennsylvania – Virginia boundaries got underway. The commissioners divided themselves into two groups of four men with the state being represented by two men in each of the groups. One group was to commence at the western end of the Mason-Dixon line and proceed eastward, while the other group commenced at the eastern end and proceeded westward. Ewing, Madison, Ellicott, and Hutchins went to the western end of the extended Mason-Dixon line. David and the remaining three men proceeded eastward to the extended line at the Delaware River.

Conflicts in the Western group surfaced almost before their trek to the western border of Pennsylvania began. Ewing and Madison were the main provocateurs with most of the group's disagreements. Based on his experience and knowledge, Ewing considered himself as the leader of the group. Madison found it hard to allow Ewing that courtesy. As far as Madison was concerned, Ewing was a petty fault finder and an obstinate and irritable individual. One of their disagreements centered on the clock Madison had brought from Virginia.

"I take umbrage with your comments about my clock not being accurate or dependable." Madison shot back at Ewing after a disdainful comment Ewing made about Madison's clock.

"It is is a very fine clock, even better than Mr. Rittenhouses." Madison retorted even though he knew his response to be untrue.

Now it was Hutchin's turn to be upset. "How dare you compare your clock, or any other clock, to the masterpieces made by Mr. Rittenhouse! His clocks are world-renowned!"

Had David known of the discourse between the three men about a clock, his modesty would compel him to dismiss it as a disagreement about nothing.

The commissioners in the eastern group maintained their civility toward one another. While the other saw David as the leader of their group, David himself did not seek that designation. When the others turn to him for help or advice he was quick to render both. His knowledge and experience were unquestioned by everyone in the group.

John Page, who had "heard much of that Great Man" was an ardent admirer of David and in fact purposely volunteered for the eastern unit so he could be placed in association with him. Page spent much time writing about David's fine qualities to Thomas Jefferson. At one time, Jefferson poked fun at Page thanking him for the information about David, telling Page he had no idea David had such fine qualities.

The weather of the summer of 1784 was very unpredictable, and David and his group could only work on their observations sparingly. During the first part of September, Page and Lukens left the team and went home, leaving only David and Robert Andrews to complete the duties still ahead for the expedition.

By mid-October David and Andrews met up with Ewing's team in the West. After verifying each other's findings they were able to determine their longitude. But before the boundary markings began, Madison also withdrew and went home. The original eight commissioners had now been cut to five commissioners.

They had hired laborers to cut away the brush and fallen trees that stood in the way of clear observations. The woods were thick with underbrush and the commissioners had been warned of the danger of getting lost in them.

One day toward the end of the expedition, David and Andrew Porter, the commissary, prepared to venture into the woods to continue their surveying, even though the foreboding sky was an omen of approaching bad weather. As they were leaving camp, one of the laborers cautioned them about the weather, and the danger of getting lost.

"We have had too many weather delays," Porter replied. "The sooner we finish our task, the sooner we will be able to go home."

"There go a couple of fools," the laborer grumbled to himself as he took a seat by the camp fire.

Almost as if preordained, David and Porter did in fact get lost in the woods that day. To worsen their situation the weather turned cold. Then it began to rain a heavy cold rain which quickly turned into snow flurries. David found a large hollowed out tree where the two men decided to hunker down in while they waited for someone in camp to realize they were late in coming back. If, after the storm passed, they may also be able to find their way back to camp by themselves.

Eventually someone at the campsite realized they were probably lost in the woods. The laborers began shooting their rifles into the air in an attempt to guide David and Porter back to camp. The strategy worked. However, by the time they made it back into camp, they were both drenched by the rain, and cold from the snow.

As they approached the camp, the laborer who had warned them not to go was leaning on his rifle and was heard muttering, "dad burn fools, those two."

After that incident the commissioners decided to halt further measurements until summer of 1785. After loading wagons with their equipment the commissioners rode ahead leaving Porter with the job of getting the equipment back home.

CHAPTER 8

Hannah was always pleased to see David return from his trips, whether it was purchasing supplies for the Army or an inspection of tax collectors' books. This time, Hannah was especially happy to see David upon his return from the border survey. As with all previous times, it was her responsibility to keep the Treasury operating smoothly in his absence. However, she had never before been involved in an election. The threat of that changing frightened her.

"I was at my wits' end and prayed with all my heart that you would return quickly," she confided in him, one evening shortly after his return. They were spending a rare evening together without interruption from David's political or scientific friends. David was sitting in his favorite easy chair, and Hannah was finishing her needlepoint of a large elm tree surrounded by flowers and birds. The elm was her favorite tree, and she had many reminders of that from artifacts placed throughout their home.

David looked up from a letter he had received while he was away. It was a letter from Thomas Jefferson informing David that he, Jefferson, had been appointed as a Minister to France in March of that year. Jefferson, never one to let a chance for a good jest go by, also made fun of David for getting lost in the woods.

"Why should that be, my dear. You have always filled in admirably for me in the past."

"I have never had a problem with making account of the funds I received, and dispersing them as I was ordered to do. However, this time, you were gone during a time of impending political turmoil. I had neither the stomach for, or the experience needed to keep your name, as you always have, my dear David, above the fray."

David looked at her with a warm and gentle smile. "I know that somehow you would have found a way to do that splendidly. I have never known you to be overwhelmed by any task that confronted you." Hannah chuckled to herself.

"That may be, my dearest, but it certainly was not a task I wanted for myself, for if I had failed, your name, which is so revered by everyone, regardless of their political persuasions, may have been slandered and smeared with mud. I did not want that responsibility to fall on my shoulders. I respect and love you too much to be the instrument of such a wretched outcome."

Hannah was right. The upcoming elections brought political upheaval and needed an experienced and steady hand to see one's way through the quagmire without getting sullied. While David's friends, the constitutionalists, had gained power in the October elections, their proposal for paying off the obligations owed to Pennsylvanians by both the state and Congress caused a firestorm of criticism and claims of legislative misconduct and speculation in the depressed securities.

One of the legislators charged with speculation was Jonathan Dickinson Sergeant, an eminent Philadelphia lawyer who had served as Pennsylvania's Attorney General from 1777 to 1780. He was also courting David's daughter, Elizabeth. After speaking with Sergeant several times about the matter, David was convinced he was innocent of all of the charges being leveled against him.

Now, more than ever, Hannah was glad that David had come home in time to wage these political battles for himself. Despite the fact that David, as Treasurer, would be the one funding the repayment plan and that everyone knew of his daughter's courtship by Sergeant, David was able to keep his name and reputation of never purchasing public securities while serving as State Treasurer intact. As a result, there was no question in anyone's mind that David was not involved.

Once again David turned to the solace of science. He did not accomplish any meaningful experiments or discover any new principle of science during this time, but he was able to relieve some of the stress of the demands put upon him by both the Treasury and the Loan Office. He also became more involved in the Philosophical Society where he worked in cooperation with Hopkinson and Vaughn in efforts on two projects.

The first project, which they were able to complete, resulted in securing a lot on State House Square upon which the new home of the Philosophical Society would be built. They even established a building fund to raise money for the construction of the building. Other projects they worked on, such as publishing the next volume of *Transactions* and installing a botanical garden on Hopkinson's lot, were not so fruitful.

Even though he had not contributed to any meaningful advance of the sciences recently, on a personal level, David was still so admired that Rev. James Madison, then president of the College of William and Mary, insisted that David accept an honorary master's degree from the College. Following much persuading by Rev. Madison and members of the Philosophical Society, David relented and accepted the honor toward the end 1784.

As for Hopkinson, he, much like Franklin, had an imagination that allowed him to envision improvements regarding apparatuses that had been invented by others. However, also much like Franklin, he did not have the mechanical, or mathematical skill to do much more than wonder if his ideas were practical. Therefore, he brought his ideas to David for perfection, just as Franklin had.

After consulting with David regarding a new method of "quilling" a harpsichord in early 1785, Hopkinson later informed Jefferson of his ideas and their perfection by David, adding he had David and several of his friends from the Philosophical Society assemble in his home to witness the effects of his new method. All of the gentlemen, he said, viewed his new method with applause.

During the time Jefferson served as Minister to France, he frequently wrote to David and other Philosophical Society associates in an attempt to keep them informed of new experiments and developments in the sciences. When those letters were not addressed to David, Jefferson always included a plea to pass the information on to David.

David, however, was unable to enjoy any platitudes directed his way. His thoughts were foremost on the remaining border measurements which were to be concluded in 1785. His original intent was to let the other commissioners survey and decide the Western border of Pennsylvania. However, it was soon apparent to David that his other commissioners wanted nothing to do with completing the job they started in 1784.

One by one they found excuses to withdraw from the 1785 expedition. Virginia was able to successfully appoint Ellicott and Colonel Joseph Nevil. Finally, Pennsylvania secured David's service as a Commissioner along with Andrew Porter and Captain Stephen Porter who was to be commissary.

As plans were being made to complete the 1784-85 measurements, David became aware that New York's Governor Clinton was pressing for an exact placement of the line between New York and Pennsylvania. Based on the assumption that New York's request could be fulfilled in 1786, Pennsylvania appointed David and Stephen Porter to establish the border between New York and Pennsylvania. New York, however, placed an immediate urgency on the matter.

Completing the two assignments that were hundreds of miles apart simultaneously was going to be an almost impossible task, one that David told Council President Dickinson would be beyond the scope of his endurance. Fortunately, one of the New York commissioners, Simeon DeWitt, wrote to Dickinson in early May, requesting a meeting with David in Philadelphia. The meeting was held at the Philosophical Society's facilities.

David and Andrew Porter met with DeWitt and another Commissioner from New York. After the introduction formalities, the four men sat down at a conference table. David opened the session with the request from the

New York delegation to postpone the New York border measurements for another year. Before David had an opportunity to explain the basis of his request, DeWitt's associate became irate.

"I know who you are," he said shaking a finger at David. David glanced at DeWitt. His face was etched with surprise and humiliation.

"Sit down man!" DeWitt bellowed at his companion. "You're making a fool of yourself and you are embarrassing me as well as the state of New York."

"What was that all about, pray tell," Andrew Porter asked. From the sound of his voice, it was clear that Porter was agitated over the outburst against David.

"All the way here, DeWitt could not stop telling me how great a scientist, surveyor, and mathematician you were. But I know you just use subterfuge and shell games in fooling people. You, and others like you, are nothing but charlatans.

David was not so egotistical or naive to believe that everyone thought of him with accolades. But neither had he been expecting such a vile discourse from a man he did not know. "My good man, we're not here to discuss whatever impressions you may have of me," David said in a soft, calm voice. "I can only suggest that if you are not prepared to work with me on this project, you ask your government to excuse you. If you think you can tolerate my presence, let us proceed."

"I have every intention of completing this assignment," the man grumbled. "Let us proceed."

After David had an opportunity to explain his request for the delay of the marking of the New York – Pennsylvania line, DeWitt agreed, over the objection of his fellow New Yorker, to request a delay from Governor Clinton. It was clear from the way DeWitt handled his companion's objections that he had little, if any, weight in any matters of significance. That pleased David for confrontation was something he did not relish and if David was right, his fellow New Yorkers would keep him in line.

David then began preparing for the expedition to finish the 1784 measurements of the western border. As usual, he made arrangements to turn the duties of the Treasury over to Hannah. He also consented to let his sister Esther's son, Benjamin Smith Barton, the brother of William Barton who had helped design the Great Seal of the United States, accompany him.

The first leg of the journey was York. The road they took was little more than a dirt path which the spring rains had turned to mush. The road, which barely qualified for such a designation, was used regularly by travelers going to and from Kentucky. A lot of the ruts in the road were deep and offered a traveler many bone breaking jolts. But David and Barton were more awed by the scenery than they were upset by the condition of the road.

After a few days travel, they arrived in York where they were met by one of David's tax collectors who handed over to him a couple of hundred pounds that he had collected. The collection of taxes reminded David that for the last three days he had been free of politics and money. Unfortunately, the euphoria did not last long, as the guilt of leaving his burdens for Hannah to bear weighed heavily upon him.

From York, they crossed the Mason-Dixon line and traveled the banks of the Potomac. They followed the Potomac for three days, all the while being inspired by the view. David became conscious of the serenity he had not felt for a long time, as he let himself be absorbed by the beauty and quiet of the nature that surrounded him.

As they approached Old Town, it started to rain, making the road muddy and treacherous. Suddenly the wagon carrying David and his nephew violently lurched to the left. Barton's grip on the seat handle slipped off the wet handle. An astonished look crossed his face as he realized he was going to be thrown from the wagon. Suddenly he felt a tug on his sleeve as he settled back down into the seat. David had realized his plight and at the last moment possible, at the risk of his own life, pulled Benjamin back into the seat. Just then they heard a large crack. A tree axle had snapped on their wagon.

It had now begun raining harder as the two men were helped down from the tilted wagon. David looked up into the sky. Nature was not being as kind of them now as it had been earlier. They both huddled under one of the wagons with some of the laborers who have been hired for the trip. The rain soon subsided into a steady, misty drizzle. The laborers were able to lift the wagon enough to get the wheel and the axle off and take it into Old Town for the necessary repairs.

At first, David was dismayed by the delay. But he soon discovered how delightful a person his young nephew was, as they scoured for rocks that were good candidates to hold fossils inside. During those three days, they cracked many rocks and found an abundance of fossils. David was surprised when Benjamin began to express an interest in the lives and histories of the local aborigines. He had long been known to be as curious as anyone in his illustrious family, including his uncle, David, but his curiosity thus far was mainly directed to natural history and botany. Fortunately the wagon axle was fixed within three days and the expedition was able to continue.

It had continuously rained for those three days and David seriously questioned the rationale for continuing the trip in the rain. He knew the creeks and streams would be swollen and that the roads would be treacherous. However, his young nephew, always ready for new adventure, persuaded David to proceed, even if it were going to be dangerous. Benjamin's and Porter's main argument was that the time would be wasted if they sat in Old Town. They had already lost three days and Barton argued that it was crucial that they not waste any more time in idleness. So amid a downpour, they continued their journey.

By the time the three men approached Wills Creek on the other side of Fort Cumberland, they had already passed through the treacherous, rain-soaked, ankle-deep mud, of the "narrows". Now they drew the wagon to a halt and stared in dismay at the swollen rushing currents of the Creek. By this time David's young nephew had had his fill of adventure. It was no longer an exciting excursion into the unknown for him. It had become a job and he wished he had not chided his uncle David into allowing him to come along. But he had, and there was no way he was going to abandon his uncle now. All of the Barton children idolized their uncle, and Benjamin was no exception. He would rather die than disappoint his uncle David.

"Well, now what do we do?" Benjamin asked as he stepped down from the wagon. "Do we make camp here until the flooding goes down?" David looked wryly at Benjamin. Porter too, was waiting for David's thoughts on the situation.

"You told me you wish to accompany me on this trip so that you might acquire some experience in the wilds. We are in the wilds, and this is the time for you to gain your sought-after experience." David said smiling at his young protege.

"I'm not sure I follow you, Uncle." Benjamin had a look on his face that belied his confusion. Never one to lose a teaching opportunity to his nephews, David continued.

"Suppose I were not along on this trip and you encountered the same dilemma as the one confronting us at this moment. Mustering all of your ingenuity, of which I know you are well endowed, decide what logical, though maybe unusual, choices you have. After you have decided on your possible choices, think through each the *pros* and the *cons* of each one. Then revisit each one and compare it to the others, until you have a workable logical solution. As I recall, we were faced with a delay at Old Town, but you thought a delay would cost us too much time. Have you now changed your mind regarding another delay?"

Benjamin had an incredulous look on his face. "Sir, you know I have always respected and admired you beyond any other man that I have ever known and it is with great humility that I reject your process. It could take a day or so to reach a solution to a problem using your thought process."

"That I believe is an exaggeration and is totally untrue. It may take a little time until you become used to the methodology, but then you'll find you can rapidly do the exercise in your mind," David replied.

"Well, my dear uncle, I do believe you are playing with me, and that you already have done the calculations that you just described. So what shall we do now?" Benjamin said with a broad grin on his face. David looked at Benjamin with a seriousness in his usually soft gray eyes.

"We wait until you have arrived at what you can postulate as a workable solution." Benjamin could tell that his uncle was taking this lesson seriously. He slowly made his way toward a fallen tree limb. The limb had been worked into a bow-like configuration by the Creek and the weather. The hump made a fine seat upon which to sit and watch the swollen river rapidly flow by and to ponder and ponder and ponder some more on a solution to its crossing. Meanwhile, Porter angrily took David aside. After David explained to Porter that he thought this was a good time to teach his nephew to think for himself, and that it would only cause a few hours delay, Porter relented.

David kept busy gathering as much dry tinder as possible. Once back at the creek-side with an appropriate amount of tinder, he lit a small fire, all the while keeping his attention directed to his nephew. Suddenly, Benjamin leaped from the log and walked toward David with an energized pace. David smiled to himself. Maybe, just maybe, he had been able to teach the young man a skill that would do him well the rest of his life.

As he approached the small campfire, David decided to let him speak first. The young man squatted down on his haunches beside his uncle and warmed himself. He then got a stick large enough to hold his wet overcoat and stuck it as far as he could into the mud. He then placed small rocks around the base of the stick to give it more support. When he was satisfied, he took off his wet overcoat, and hung it by the fire. David watched him all the time but did not say a word.

The lad once again squatted down on his haunches to warm himself by the fire. Neither he or David said a word for several minutes. Finally, Benjamin broke the silence, "How would you like to help me build a canoe, Uncle David?" Porter shot a bewildering look at David.

David had never built a canoe before but out of curiosity he had studied various Indian methods of building such a craft. He was confident he could help build one sufficient enough to cross the river and its swiftly moving current. He did not relay that confidence to his nephew, however. He simply looked at him and asked, "What about the wagon, the instruments, and our supplies?"

Young Benjamin smiled, for he had thought about that as well. "First, we break the wagon down and put it part by part on a raft Then, we float everything across the river on the raft. Of course, someone will have to paddle the canoe while the others pull the raft behind the canoe with ropes."

David nodded as he briefly mulled the plan over in his mind. "Why not eliminate the canoe and we all go over on the raft?" David asked. He knew the answer to that question and asked it just to see if Benjamin had thought about it.

To David's delight, his young pupil had a ready answer. "Because we would have to pole the raft across the river. The rapids are so strong that there is a very good possibility that one, or all three of us would not be able to control our pole, and we would be swept into the river".

David glanced at Porter. "Your thoughts, Andrew?"

"Well we still have enough daylight to put your plan into effect, so perhaps we should start collecting the resources we need," Porter said, smiling at David.

David reached out and shook Porter's hand. "Now, that boy is extremely intelligent," Porter told David. Benjamin had a pleased look on his young face as he went about his chores.

It took the three men about an hour to gather the materials they needed. David and Porter gave Benjamin instructions on how to construct a canoe sufficient enough to get them across the river, while they began strapping the raft together. In addition to making the canoe, Benjamin also hewed two paddles from a couple of small uprooted trees.

Within two hours the two vessels were ready for the river. All that remained was to dismantle the wagon enough to be transported across the river along with their supplies and equipment. Within half an hour they had the raft loaded, but they had no time to waste, it would soon be dark.

It was decided that Benjamin, the strongest of the trio, would paddle the canoe, while David and Porter attended to the guide ropes on the raft. It was crucial for the raft to be held as even with the canoe as possible. If the raft became caught in the swiftly moving rapids, it could tangle itself in the brush along the creek bank. Even worse, it could end up turning the canoe around so that it was facing the bank it had come from. If the men had to change positions while in the rapids, one or all three could end up drowned.

It was with a little *angst* that they took their positions in the canoe. Benjamin sat a little forward of the central point of the canoe, while David and Porter sat to the rear, facing the raft. There was little doubt in David's mind that Benjamin was strong enough to paddle the canoe across the current to the other side. What troubled him was the uncertainty of his ability to hold the ropes of the raft steady enough. While he had a lot of stamina, he did not have a lot of upper body strength, and they had a treacherous 30 yards to make it to the other side.

As they started to cross the waters, the shallows were fairly calm which made paddling the canoe an easy task. Benjamin, assuming that the rest of the passage would be as easy, relaxed his grip on the paddle. Suddenly and without warning, the canoe was in the fastest part of the rapids. Almost immediately, Benjamin's paddle was forcefully torn from his hand. He reached for the second paddle, but could not find it. Within ten seconds, the canoe and the raft were raging down the creek out of control. Benjamin tried frantically to find the second paddle but he still couldn't find it.

Suddenly Porter spotted the paddle in the back of the canoe and pushed it forward to Benjamin but he had to stand up in order to do so. The canoe began to tip to one side. Both David and Benjamin shifted their weights to steady the canoe, while Porter tried to sit back down.

As Benjamin steadied the canoe, the force of the quick change in direction sent David flying into the creek. Fortunately, he had looped the rope to the raft around his back so it would be easier for him to guide the ropes. As David began to tumble and lose control of his movements in the current, he reached out with one hand and grabbed the side of the canoe.

Benjamin started to make a movement to help David. David quickly waved him back and told him to "paddle, paddle, I'm fine".

As they approached the far side of the creek, Benjamin realized that the spot that they had picked out as the best spot to land was no longer in sight, and he no longer had the strength to paddle upstream against the rapids. Then he spotted a small clearing. He frantically paddled the canoe toward it. Once he had beached the canoe, he ran back into the water to assist his uncle in his attempt to stand. Once he had David on his feet, he took the ropes away from him and motioned for him to go dry land.

By the time the men had crossed the creek, it was too dark to reassemble the wagon. While David changed into warm clothing, Benjamin gathered enough wood to make a large fire so David and he could dry their wet clothes. After the fire had been going for a while, David lit a large stick with some burlap wrapped around one end. The flame from the make-shift torch was sufficient to allow the men to check their supplies and instruments. They were relieved when their cursory inspection failed to find any damage.

The next morning, they were greeted by a typical Philadelphia spring day. Their breakfast was eaten under a sunny blue sky with an occasional fluffy cloud casting a shadow on them for a moment or two. All of the men had a feeling that the nice weather was a good omen for the rest of the excursion, even David. While the scientist in him knew that one weather phenomenon does not predict the occurrence of another totally unrelated phenomenon, he decided to put science aside for a few moments and joined in the jubilation of the other men. After checking out their supplies and instruments, they reassembled the wagon and set out for Beesontown, which was destined to be renamed Uniontown.

The men's jubilation and talk of a good omen soon faded when they heard a large crack from front axle of the wagon. The road had been damaged so badly that deep ruts not only ran parallel with the road, but also across the road. Once again, the men disassembled the wagon, and loaded it and their supplies and equipment on a sleigh which they pulled and pushed to the next settlement.

"I have never known one mile to be such a difficult journey," Barton said, as he sat exhausted on a tree stump and watched the axle being fixed. Porter and David were quick to tease the young man. If two old men could make, surely a young buck like Benjamin could, too.

"David, I thought you had a strong strapping young man for a nephew. Now it seems he is older than we are," Porter said jovially. Soon all three of them had joined in the mirth. Porter stayed with the wagon while it was being fixed. David and Benjamin took this opportunity to scour the area for fossils. To their chagrin they found none, but their discouragement vanished when they found the axle did not take long to be fixed. They were quickly on their way.

When they finally arrived in Beesontown, the Virginians were eagerly awaiting their arrival. Ellicott, who felt he had no peers in his group, was delighted to once again have the company of his friend, David. Now he was someone with whom he could carry on an intelligent conversation. The rest of the afternoon and early evening was given to high spirits and amusement.

The next day the commissioners left Beesontown, and journeyed in two separate groups to the previously marked corner of Pennsylvania. Once both groups were reunited, they immediately commenced the tedious job of making the astronomical observations, thereby gathering the data they would need to precisely mark the boundary line. While the job was tedious, David felt exhilarated while in the woods. With the burdens of the Treasury temporarily lifted from his shoulders, he slept better, and the pain from his ulcers had subsided. He found great joy in studying nature, both fauna and flora, with his nephew.

By August 23, 1785, they reached their final destination on the Ohio River, where they signed a joint certificate authenticating that they had completed the line up to that point. With their task completed, some of the commissioners began their trek home. Some, including David, decided to stay a little longer.

On September 12, David decided that he too had to leave for home. The others in the camp tried to convince him to stay, but to no avail. David left for home pleased in knowing he had done his job well. The glowing reports by others of the excursion centered mainly on David. In those reports, he was called "The Great Mr. Rittenhouse". Another report by General Richard Butler referred to the boundary line as "the line, which Mr. Rittenhouse and his assistants have run". Butler declared that the line was an example of David's outstanding judgment and wisdom, and [will] would forever be a monument to him. The line was so correct that an inspection revealed it varied only 1/10 of an inch in a 40-mile stretch.

CHAPTER 9

When David returned home, about September 25, 1785, he was greeted with the preparation of major festivities in honor of his old friend, Benjamin Franklin, who was returning from France. Because of his absence, David had not been able to participate in planning any of the events honoring Philadelphia's most famous person, and that dulled his desire to do anything but observe the various events from afar.

The American Philosophical Society planned a large event in honor of its returning president. However, the choice of the opening speaker was not a popular one. Chief Justice McKean pompously delivered a speech full of compliments to Franklin that had little depth, especially for the scientifically inclined members.

David, while as upset as most of the members, kept his own counsel. His silence on the matter was especially evident in a letter he wrote the next day to his dear friend, Thomas Jefferson, who had replaced Franklin in Paris. David did not mention either Franklin or McKean in his letter, and only congratulating Jefferson on his new position.

One of the rising concerns of David, and George Washington's was the partisan approach to all of the government's problems. The antagonism between factions had become mean-spirited and focused only on their ideological point of view. All of the factions were now jousting for a piece of Benjamin Franklin.

The Constitutionalists and the Mechanical Society, which most of the time agreed with the Constitutionals, assumed Franklin favored their cause because he had sat in on the writing of the Declaration of Independence in 1776 and also, Franklin still considered himself a mechanic. The Republicans, on the other hand, believed Franklin would side with them because he had voiced concurrence with a few of their tenets. All factions were pushing Franklin to run for a seat on the Council.

Franklin finally decided to align himself with the Constitutionalists. After he was elected, all of the factions almost unanimously urged him to become a candidate for the Presidency of the Council. It was hoped by all that he could lead the Council away from partisanship. In many ways, Franklin was able to accomplish that.

Soon, David, Pennsylvania and the country were prospering. David was now collecting more revenue for the state than he had ever been able to collect. As a result, he was rewarded handsomely with increases in pay. However, his work was still harrowing on him and his health was declining. As a result he was fond of saying he was "neither absolutely well or absolutely ill."

Life was becoming a little easier for David. He bought a lot on the northwest corner of Seventh and Mulberry Streets. Within a short time, he had erected a large, well-designed, three-story on the lot, commissioned by Joseph Ogilby. The house was built of red and black brick, which were placed alternately. It was soon being called the "Rittenhouse Mansion", and would later be deemed, "Fort Rittenhouse". It was an era in which the country was in depression and Americans were suffering, or the economy was booming and the people were happy and well- fed and clothed, depending on which experts you believed.

David and his family were counted among the optimists. Those who frequently visited with David at his residence were absorbed in philosophical conversations with David, his wife, as well as his daughters. They all received compliments on their good sense, their good nature, and their wisdom.

By 1786, one of the things David thoroughly enjoyed was gathering with Hopkinson at Franklin's residence for a "… pleasing philosophical Party." Thomas Jefferson, who was now in Paris, often wrote how much he coveted being able to partake in one of those sessions, saying he would rather sit in on one of those sessions than spend a whole week in Paris.

The American Philosophical Society was becoming so active that it finally was able to publish the second volume of *Transactions*. According to many, it is this volume that contained David's most significant experimental endeavors. It included his experiments in magnetism, his innovative research on the illusion of reversible relief and perhaps his most stunning work, which he attributed to the inquiring mind of Francis Hopkinson.

Hopkinson had also observed that when you look through a fine silk handkerchief with light in the background, you could see dark lines which did not move when he moved the handkerchief.

Hopkins, of course, wanted to know if David knew why this occurred. David did not. So he began experiments on the phenomenon. His experiments resulted in identifying the phenomenon as a diffraction of light as it passed through the handkerchief, and his paper, *"An optical problem, proposed by Mr. Hopkinson, and solved by Mr. Rittenhouse"* was published in volume 2 of Transactions.

Had he taken his inquiry one more step, he would've realized he was on the verge of discovering the wave lengths of colors. His papers on this research were well received not only in America, but also in Europe.

Unfortunately, before the newest volume of *Transactions* was actually printed, David became engaged for two more surveys. Again, the request was to complete them in the same time. Late in 1785, The American Congress appointed David, and Thomas Hutchins to determine the boundary line between New York and Massachusetts. He still had yet to help determine the boundary between New York and Philadelphia, the project that had already been deferred for a year. Again, there were two projects competing for his time and energy, but only one could be completed at a time. After meetings in Philadelphia with all the commissioners assigned to the two projects, it was cordially decided that the Pennsylvania-New York line should be completed prior to the New York- Massachusetts boundary.

Ellicott left ten days before David, who departed Philadelphia on June 27, 1786. The two men reunited at Easton, then traveled through Wind Gap, heading toward Tioga on the Susquehanna River. David was pleasantly surprised to find a harmonious community comprised of whites and Indians living there. David often expressed his belief that the races, no matter the color, should live in harmony with each other. They decided to stay in Tioga for a few days to explore the natural history of the area. After a few days, they moved on to their destination.

About five days later, they met with the New York commissioners near the spot on the West Bank of the Delaware, where Samuel Holland had marked the forty-second parallel twelve years earlier. For the next two weeks or so, they made nightly observations and determined with exactitude, that in fact, the old marker was incorrect. They relocated it a little north of where it was originally. Because the celestial observations had to be made at night, many of which were cloudy and overcast, David and his fellow commissioners were drenched in forced idleness.

David used the idle time to examine the natural history of the region. He even had occasion to think that his nephew would have enjoyed this trip more than the last expedition, for the commissioners made friends with members of the tiny Onondaga Indian community in Chenango. Their friendship was forged mainly between themselves and two daughters of the tribe's primary chief.

The daughters, Sally and Jacowe, had been sent to the commissioner's' camp to ask for food. In exchange, they would bring fresh fish and vegetables. The oldest of the daughters was Sally, who appeared to be about twenty years old. She was strikingly good-looking and "... extremely well dressed", according to David. One of the commissioners made a drawing of her which David wanted to show to Hannah. Ellicott wanted the picture turned into a large portrait.

On the second night of their friendship, the girls began singing hymns to the commissioners. It seems the whole tribe had been converted to

Christianity by the Anglicans. David knew that this was an opportunity that his nephew, Benjamin, would be sorry to have missed. Benjamin, on his uncle's advice, was preparing to transfer to the University of Edinburgh.

With their mission completed by October 12, 1786, all of the commissioners were anxious to get home. David was anxious to get home for a couple of reasons. One was that the wife of his nephew, William Barton, the former Elizabeth Rhea, was about to deliver a child, which would be David's great niece or nephew. As for David, he decided that it was the last time he was going to do any major surveying.

When David arrived back in Philadelphia, he was pleasantly surprised to find a new outlet for his papers which he felt were not appropriate, or significant enough for "*Transactions*". While he was gone, the initial volume of the *Columbian Magazine* had been published. David immediately began submitting all of his material on natural history. Since the articles were not scientifically significant, he decided to publish them anonymously.

On November 17, David's great nephew, William Barton, Jr. was born.

By the end of 1786, life had become fairly routine for David.

In the early part of 1787, David was selected vice president of the American Philosophical Society, which had entered a new phase of constant activity. At the behest of his nephew William Barton, David reviewed his thesis "*The true interests of the United States and particularly of Pennsylvania considered with Respect to the Advantages Resulting from a State Paper Money*" which was published later that year. Philadelphia was once again stimulating David's scientific senses and curiosities.

However, he still had one boundary line commitment to complete: the New York – Massachusetts boundary line. Reluctantly, David left in July 1787 to complete his last boundary line. Fortunately, this expedition only lasted for a month. When he returned home, he announced what he had determined a year before -- that he would "bid *adieu* forever to all running of lines". It was a promise he never broke.

During the month he was gone, a significant new development occurred. It was one that at first seemed to offer more prestige and praise for David. Unfortunately, it turned out to be a bitter pill which David refused to swallow. That pill was Tench Coxe.

Tench Coxe was a merchant when the Revolutionary War began. He found it easier to remain neutral, but did sympathize for the Royalists. It was rumored that he left Philadelphia, and joined the British Army under General Howe. Upon his return, he was listed as being accused of treasohad his own opinions towards America's economy, and her future.

In August, 1787, Tench Coxe wished to start a society, Encouragement of Manufacturers and the Useful Arts. As an ardent admirer of David, and a fellow Republican, Coxe was able to garner much of his support by invoking David's name as an example of the ingenuity of Americans, both as a craftsman and a scientist. As a result, the organization got off to a rousing start. At the organizational meeting, David was, without any opposition, nominated for the presidency. Before the election, however, a covert slate of officers was formed which nominated Thomas Mifflin as president. It was clear from the names on the second slate that the Bank of North America investors wanted to control the new organization.

Since everyone believed the election was perfunctory and that David would easily be elected president, voting turnout was minimal, and the clandestine slate of officers was elected. David was elected vice president but it was an honor he and his friends felt was a hollow gesture. Throughout the year he held the office, he did not partake in any of the activities of the organization and refused to stand for re-election when his term had expired.

At a time of national political unrest, the economic condition of the country was disastrous. This led to several uprisings by farmers from the western part of the states who were losing their farms to bankruptcy. In addition, there were many people, mainly Federalists, who believed that the Articles of Confederation needed to be replaced with a Constitution providing for a stronger federal government. Others believed that it could be done by amending the current Constitution.

David was among those Republicans who believed that a stronger federal government would lead to tyranny and oppression because it would shift the power from the states and the people, to a few wealthy politicians and bureaucrats. However, it was a time when the Republicans were diminishing in power, and David and his friends throughout the country were unable to stop the political onslaught of the federalists.

On September 17, 1787, the new Constitution of the United States of America was signed by thirty-eight of forty-one delegates present at a convention. The delegates' duty to draft a new constitution had been met. It was quickly ratified by five states. The non-signing states wanted further assurances and language protecting the state rights to possess any powers not delegated to the federal government.

They also wanted the protection of individual freedoms, such as freedom of speech, press, and religion. They were also vehemently opposed to the lack of a statement guaranteeing the people's rights to keep and bear arms. The reasoning behind the last right was that should the government become tyrannical, people would have the means of defending themselves from it, and would have the power to abolish the government in that event.

On July 2, 1788, the Constitution of the United States of America became the law of the land, but David and thousands of others had mixed emotions about the new Constitution. On the one hand, he shivered at the thought of a strong centralized national government sapping power from the states. On the other hand, he was very pleased that amendments to the Constitution protecting states' rights as well as the right to freedom of religion, freedom of the press, and the right to keep and bear arms would be forthcoming. He had no idea that even with those protections, the federal government would slowly erode individual rights, as well as the states' rights recognized in those amendments.

One thing that did depress David was that his beloved Philadelphia would no longer be the capital of the United States. Congress decided that New York would be the seat of the new federal government. However, in December 1788, Maryland was pushing for the federal capital to be in a territory uncontrolled by any state, and was prepared to cede part of its state to the federal government for that purpose.

But, all in all, David had reached a point in life and his career that he was happier than he had been in a long, long time. Accolades were coming not only from America, but also from Europe. Men of distinction and accomplishment were eager to seek out David whenever they were near Philadelphia.

With the first American presidential election coming up beginning on December 15, 1788, David was placed on the Electoral College ballot by his constitutionalist friends. He would lose the election on January 10, 1789. However, there was one election that was won that David was grateful for" William Barton, Sr. was elected to the American Philosophical Society.

In April 6, 1789, David's dear friend, George Washington, became the unanimous choice of the Electoral College to be the first President of the United States of America. John Adams was elected the first Vice President. The political climate throughout the nation was in a state of uncertainty, and Pennsylvania did not escape the turmoil.

David decided amid the mounting pressures that it would be best if he resigned as Treasurer of the state of Pennsylvania. About that time, his nephew, Benjamin Smith Barton, returned from his studies in Europe and began practicing medicine in Philadelphia. Meanwhile, his nephew, William Barton, the designer of the great seal of the United States, was appointed by President Washington as the Judge of the Western Territory. Barton declined the nomination.

David was pleased to see Congress follow through on the promise to add amendments to the U.S. Constitution. All in all, twelve amendments were sent to the states for ratification. However, only ten were ratified.

On April 17, 1790, Benjamin Franklin passed away. David became depressed. He and Franklin had been close dear friends for forty years. He had been through the revolution together and had achieved a common goal, to make America a free country whose government's primary role was the interests of the people it served. Their names were often linked when one spoke of American progress in the sciences. As a token of their, friendship Franklin left his reflecting telescope to David.

Approximately 20,000 people showed up for Franklin's funeral. It was considered an honor of great magnitude to be a pallbearer. His six pall bearers were: Pennsylvania's President, Thomas Mifflin; the Chief Justice of the State Supreme Court, Thomas McKean; the President of the Bank of North America, Thomas Willing; The Mayor of Philadelphia, Samuel Powell; the city's leading economic personality, William Bingham; and David.

David was pleased by the return of the nation's Capital to Philadelphia that summer. No one knew for how long it would remain the nation's Capital, for Congress had voted to build a new Capital on a 10 mi.^{2} site from land contributed by Maryland and Virginia. The site chosen was currently swamp land and had to be surveyed before a city could be constructed. Using some equipment made for him by David, and his brother Benjamin, Major Andrew Ellicott and his new assistant, a self-taught free Negro named Benjamin Banneker, began the job of surveying the new territory in preparation building a new federal Capital.

But for the moment, David was enjoying the Capital's relocation to Philadelphia. His circle of friends became larger and more notable. He had introduced his second daughter, Esther, who was also known as Hetty, to a young physician, Dr. Nicholas B. Waters. David had taken a liking to him, and had even sponsored his membership into the American Philosophical Society. The two married on October 22, 1790, at the Rittenhouse Mansion, and moved in with David and Hannah. His other daughter, Elizabeth, and her husband, Jonathan Dickinson Sergeant, who was the first Attorney General of Pennsylvania, lived a couple of houses down on Mulberry Street. At that time, the Sergeants had one child, a daughter named Esther Rittenhouse Sergeant.

David's nephew, Benjamin Smith Barton, was elected to a fellowship at Philadelphia's College of Physicians. He also became a professor of botany and natural history at the College of Philadelphia.

About November 12, Benjamin Smith Barton's younger brother, Richard Peters Barton, married Martha Walker of Dinwiddie County, Virginia, and moved to Virginia. Martha's father was a prominent doctor there, and she did not want to leave her family. The area of Virginia where his wife's family was located reminded Barton of his birthplace of Lancaster County, PA.

On December 15, Maria Rittenhouse was born to Jacob (Gerhard, Peter, Gerhard, Wilhelm) in North Hampton, PA.

One major thing from David's tenure as Treasurer was still bothering him. A legal case involving the sloop *Active*, in which he was involved in 1779, and was still pending before the Admiralty Court. The Court had ordered David, as State Treasurer, to post a £22,000 bond. The court still held the bond, and David wanted to be released. He took his grievance to the Council's President with a demand to be released from the case. His pleas went unanswered, and the return of the bond would remain a burden upon this estate until 1809.

At the January 1791 meeting of the American Philosophical Society, David was elected as its second president. For the two years prior to this, the Society had been languishing in member inactivity. David himself had only attended about three meetings the past year. Once he became president, that all began to change. Backed by his ardent admirers, such as Thomas Jefferson, Charles Wilson Peale, James Madison and of course his nephews, William and Benjamin Smith Barton, members of the Society began attending the meetings more regularly. Even Alexander Hamilton became a member. David was now widely referred to as 'Dr. David Rittenhouse, President of the American Philosophical Society.'

As if almost overnight, David's opinions were widely sought on a myriad of governmental projects including canal systems, highway systems, and the founding of new cities in the western part of the state. His name was even invoked in disputes over surveying work done by others, especially if they involved work that David had previously completed. If challenges arose concerning measurements or finding, all that need be said was that they were working with calculations provided by David. His advice and approval were sought at every turn especially in scientific and technological projects.

David, now considered unique by his fellow citizens, and was appointed to several honorary positions. George Washington even appointed him to receive subscriptions to the newly chartered Bank of the United States. With all of this swirling about him, David still found time for astronomical observations of which he would keep detailed notes. He was in constant communication with astronomers in Europe and elsewhere who considered him their peer.

Sadly, David's cousin Peter Rittenhouse (William, Gerhard, Wilhelm) died in Hunterdon, N. J. in 1791. New Jersey would also become the birth state to Ann Rittenhouse, who was born that year to Joseph S. Rittenhouse (Lott, William, Gerhard, Wilhelm).

On April 2, 1792, the United States Congress passed the Coinage Act, which established the United States mint. The United States never had minted coinage before. It had always used various European coins or Spanish coins. Prior to its establishment, David had been consulted regarding the machinery which would be needed for the mint. He, therefore, seemed the logical choice to become the country's first Secretary of the Mint. While he was appointed by President George Washington, he reported directly to Thomas Jefferson as the Secretary of State, rather than Alexander Hamilton, the Secretary of the Treasury.

But, first things first, the mint machinery had to be built and David knew just the man for that job. He called his old friend, Henry Voigt, with whom he had worked on many projects. Conveniently, Voigt had worked at mints in Germany. He was hired immediately by David as chief coiner and engraver.

David began looking for a building to house the mint. He found the perfect site on the corner of 7th Street and Filbert, which was an old abandoned distillery. After demolishing the building, David laid the cornerstone for the new United States federal mint that summer. The building would be referred as, "Ye Olde Mint", and was not only the tallest building in Philadelphia, being at 3 stories tall, but also the first federal building erected under the Constitution.

However, the mint did not begin operation until October, and then only after three coining presses had been received from Europe.

On December 15, Maria Rittenhouse was born to Jacob (Gerhard, Peter, Gerhard, Wilhelm) in North Hampton, PA.

In the early part of 1792, Richard Peters Barton's wife, Martha, delivered the couples first child, Robert Barton, in the Valley of Virginia, which was just south of Winchester, VA.

The relationship between David and Jefferson became more solidified than ever before. Early in 1793, Jefferson had occasion to present the bust of himself, made while he was in France, to David, saying "I doubt very much its usefulness, but nonetheless, I want you have it as a token of my great esteem for you." Needless to say, David was extremely touched by the gift. He told Jefferson that to him, "It is more acceptable than any other thing of its kind in existence".

That evening, David, while scanning the night skies, discovered a new comet. The excitement of the discovery kept David in constant observation of its trip across one constellation to another. He kept meticulous notes on its path hoping to be able to reconstruct its orbit. Meanwhile, David's brother Benjamin married his second wife, Francis Wade, on January 22.

Unfortunately, he was not able to see the comet after February 8, 1793. Many people later blamed the comet for an assortment of evils that befell the United States, Europe, and even Philadelphia.

At home, political parties and partisanship were on the rise. The French Revolution was applauded by some Americans, while others found the French revolutionaries' proclivity for torture and brutalization of their fellow Frenchmen as abhorrent and inhumane. Societies and clubs were formed to express the sentiments of those supporting the French Revolution and its aftermath. One of the most powerful was the Democratic Society of Pennsylvania, so named because they advocated spreading democracy throughout Europe.

The Pennsylvania Society was initially formed by Hutchinson, Jonathan Dickinson Sergeant (David's son-in-law), and a few others. At the meeting to elect a list of officers, David was the unequivocal choice for president. David did not accept or decline the group's presidency, and he never attended any of its meetings. By midsummer, everyone's focus in Philadelphia turned to one mutual enemy: yellow fever..

"We must decide what we are going to do while this plague passes over the city," David said, addressing his close family members during a family summit at the family home. Present were David's daughter, Elizabeth, who was referred to as 'Betsy'; her husband Jonathan Dickinson Sergeant, and their children, four-year-old Esther and two-year-old David; David's youngest daughter Esther, whom everyone called 'Hetty', her husband, Dr. Nicholas Waters, and their two-year-old son, also named David. They were all gathered around David and Hannah's large oak dining table that sat in the couple's formal dining room, just off the family kitchen and the foray. Betsy was just weeks away from delivering her third child.

"As a doctor, it is my duty to stay, to help the best I can, although I must say we have no known remedies. It is more a matter of comforting the patients, and doing the best we can. Hopefully, we will be able to save a few lives," Nicholas said. He had been pacing the floor, as if his decision had been troubling to him. He now stood behind his wife, Hetty, and gently placed his hands on her shoulders. "However, Hetty and little David are not bound by my Hippocratic oath. It is my wish that they leave immediately."

Jonathan was next to speak. "I, like Nicholas, feel duty bound to stay, as yesterday I accepted an appointment to the Mayor's committee to seek ways to maintain a modicum of order during this crisis. We will be meeting on a daily basis. One of our concerns is establishing more space to treat those afflicted with the fever."

Betsy gasped. "Why did you did not consult me about this first? You know I am a few weeks away from delivering our third child. I do not want to have it born without a father! If you stay there is no guarantee that you, yourself will survive. What am I to do then? Raise three small children by myself?"

Her husband gave her a stern look. "Why must you always look at the dark side of things, my dear? I shall survive, but you, as close to childbirth as you are, are much more vulnerable to this fever than I. That is why I must demand that you leave the city as soon as possible. From all estimates, the danger should be passed within three or four months."

"You can demand all you want, Jonathan, but I will tell you this, if you are staying then I am staying." Jonathan's look now turned to consternation.

Then, David spoke. "Well, it seems that the three of us all have civic duties which call for us to remain as long as possible in the city. There are duties I must take care of at the mint to make sure it is up and running as quickly as possible. Therefore, this is my suggestion...All of the women, and children prepare to leave for the farm in Norritown. I will see all of you there safely and return to the city to complete my duties at the mint."

"I will have none of that," Hannah said indignantly. "Betsy has already stated that if Jonathan is going to stay, she is going to stay with him, and I will not let my daughter go through this childbirth without me at her side."

The family finally decided that the David and Jonathan were going to stay in the city to fulfill their duties to the local and federal governments, while Nicholas would fulfill his duty under his allegiance to his Hippocratic oath. Against Jonathan's will, Betsy was also going to stay, at least until her child was born. Hannah was going to stay to see Betsy through her childbirth. David would take Hetty and little David to the farm.

By the end of August, over thirty-five percent of the residence of Philadelphia had fled the city. City government, the federal government, and the state government were all in turmoil as legislators and bureaucrats departed the city. The streets and the roads leading out of the city were clogged with those who were fleeing. The city was in chaos and bedlam. Dr. Waters worked almost around the clock, and was in constant contact with Sergeant to inform him of supplies and medicines that the doctors needed. In addition, Sergeant was busy trying to find make-shift hospital space for the overflow of patients. Unfortunately, on October 5, 1793, Jonathan Dickinson Sergeant fell ill with the fever himself. He was placed under the care of his brother-in-law, Nicholas.

CHAPTER 10

Nicholas came home after three days of attending to the ill in two makeshift hospitals without sleep. He was greeted at the door by David and Hannah's maid. He was ready to collapse, but before he could rest there was something he had to do.

"Where is Miss Hannah?" he asked in a soft gentle tone that was almost a whisper.

The maid could tell from looking at Nicholas that he was exhausted and she could tell from the tone of his voice that he had bad news to tell Miss Hannah. He and Hetty had been living there for almost three years and she had gotten to know his little nuances.

"She is in Miss Betsy's room. I'll fetch her for if you would like me to." She said. "Yes, yes, please. I must speak with her before I lie down." He said. His voice had a sense of urgency. "I will be in the kitchen making some tea." He told her as she walked from the room.

He was soon joined in the kitchen by Hannah, and it was obvious from the look on her face that the maid had relayed his sense of urgency to Hannah. She walked over to where he was seated. He arose when he realized she had come into the room. His beleaguered face told her all she had to know. "It's about Jonathan, isn't it?"

"Yes, ma'am. He passed away a couple of hours ago. I wanted to talk to you first before telling Betsy." Hannah started to let out a large gasp, but was able to muffle it with her hand. "I didn't know how strong she is being this close to labor." he added. "I don't believe that she is any closer than two weeks," Hannah said as she sat down at the table beside Nicholas. She gently put her hand on Nicholas's forearm. "And we certainly can't wait two weeks to tell her. How is your bedside manner?"

As a Doctor Nicholas had to give bad news to patients or their relatives in the past, so this was nothing new to him. What was new is that in the past he barely knew the people he was dealing with. Now he must tell his sister-in-law that her worst fears had happened. He really hoped that Hannah would be able to bear that burden.

Nicholas looked up at the ceiling and sighed deeply. "If you would kindly tell her that I would like to speak with her so as to prepare her for my intrusion into the chambers, I would appreciate it."

Nicholas watched Hannah leave the room before he buried his head in his hands. He was exhausted from three nights and days at the hospital, but before he got any rest he would have to tell a person he truly admired that she would never see her husband alive again.

Betsy took the news of Jonathan's passing extremely hard. At first, she blamed herself for not insisting that they leave the city. She recalled over and over in her mind the conversation the family had at the dining table a few weeks earlier. She was convinced that if she had not said anything to Jonathan about dying and leaving his kids without a father, that he would still be alive. Hannah was finally able to convince her that what she said at the table that night had nothing to do with Jonathan's death.

By November, 17,000 people in the city were able to make their way back home. Of the 38,000 Pennsylvanians who had remained in the vicinity, a little over 4,000, or twelve percent of the population, had succumbed to the fever. One of those was Joseph Wright, David's engraver at the mint. Just before his death, Wright had engraved the dies of one cent and half cent copper coins. David's plan for the coining of silver and gold pieces had to be delayed by the shortage and price of both. However, he was able to proceed with the copper coins which was a huge success. To add to his woes, David was informed by Jefferson in November that he planned to resign his position as Secretary of State in a couple of months.

At the beginning of January, David was re-elected president of the Democratic Society, as well as president of The American Philosophical Society. However, he was becoming somewhat suspicious of the Democratic Society's stances against the federal government. He felt that as long as he was a part of the Mint, he would be remiss to be a member let alone president of an organization that was anti-federal government. It quickly became apparent to him that the Democratic Society was going in a direction he did not wish to endorse, and he resigned as president.

David spent little time in his observatory and workshop. And the time he did spend in them, he produced nothing of real lasting value to the scientific community. Most of his time was committed to the Mint, and canal projects. His main political allies were either dead, had removed themselves from office, or were under heavy fire by their opponents. And the Society itself was having difficulty recovering from the fever.

One of the bright sides of David's life during this time was his friendship with Giuseppe Ceracchi, an Italian sculptor who came to the United States on a visit to build a monument commemorating America's revolution. David took Ceracchi with him on a couple of inspections of projects that he was responsible for, but soon it became apparent to Ceracchi that he would be unable to build his monument at any of the locations. Instead, Ceracchi carved a bust of David, and gave it to the Philosophical Society.

By the summer of 1794, the city was once again struck with yellow fever. Fortunately, it was not nearly as severe as previous year's epidemic. Unrelated to the outbreak of yellow fever, Hetty's husband, Nicholas Waters, died of a respiratory problem that summer, making both of David's daughters widows within a year.

All the while, David was enduring his problems at the Mint. In some cases, he was refused permission to expand the Mint's facilities. In others, if his audit of the Mint's books revealed a shortage, he would cover the shortage out of his own salary. In other cases, if he felt certain items purchased by the Mint were too costly, he would pay for them himself.

All this was not enough however, and soon the Mint was being criticized by Congress and the business community alike. It was to the point, that a congressional investigation was deemed appropriate. An investigation was initiated resulting in three or four reports being made to Congress. In the end, David was exonerated of any wrongdoing or malfeasance of his duties, but once all the reports were in he promptly submitted his resignation effective June 30, 1795.

By now his health and his stomach for all the controversy were both dwindling and he began withdrawing from a life that at times he endured and at other times reveled in. He remained mostly at home, content in sharing his time and life with his family. He even curtailed his attendance at meetings of the Philosophical Society.

Both of his daughter's, and their children moved into the big house with David and Hannah, and provided a life that by no means was secluded and quiet. Betsy had three children, a boy, and two girls, while Hetty had one child, a boy. Both Betsy and Hetty had named their sons, now both four years old, David Rittenhouse. At times anarchy seemed to rain supreme. But, David loved every minute of it.

In the summer of that year, David was elected to the Royal Society of London, perhaps the finest tribute from the most highly regarded scientific academy of the English-speaking world. He confided in Hannah that it was his most prized accolade. David was only the second American scientist elected to the Society.

In April 1796, David's most enduring friend still alive, Thomas Jefferson, announced to David that he was going to run for president of the United States, and wanted David to run as a presidential elector for him. Unfortunately, David would not live long enough to see that happen. He did live long enough to be presented with a dissertation written on a subject that had long fascinated him. He also lived long enough to see one of his youngest nephews, Matthias Barton, a son of Reverend Thomas Barton and David's sister Esther, elected to the Pennsylvania Senate. Politics were not new to Barton. He had been a member of the state General Assembly for the previous three years.

As David's doctor, William Smith Barton, was the one person who knew how fragile his health had become. He wanted to cheer his uncle's final days, so he wrote his *Memoir Concerning the Fascinating Faculty Which has been Ascribed to the Rattle-Snake*. He presented it to his uncle on June 18.

Then on June 22, David became seriously ill and asked that his nephew Benjamin Smith Barton, who earlier that year became Professor of Materia at the University of Pennsylvania, be called to attend to him. On June 23, Barton requested a consultation regarding David's illness with Dr. Adam Kuhn, and David's lawyer began to write a will for him.

For the next couple of days, David displayed unusual irritability, especially, about things that Hannah did, which was uncommon and out of character for him. On the evening of June 25, his pain became more severe than ever before, and even an external application of a compress of meal and opium could not dull the pain. A few hours later Barton checked in with David to see if he felt more comfortable. With a softness in David's gray eyes that Barton had never seen before, David managed a faint smile. He took Barton's hand and replied in a weak voice "Yes, you have made the way to God easier."

A few hours later, David became so delirious that Hannah could not bear to watch his misery. At ten minutes to two in the morning, on June 26, 1796, with his nephew Benjamin Smith Barton, and his daughter Hetty at his side, David drew his last breath. Soon after his death, John Rhea Barton (William Barton & Esther Rittenhouse, Mathias, Nicholas, Wilhelm) was born in Lancaster.

David's funeral service would be held in the garden next to what would become his mausoleum, his observatory. His name, time of death, and his age were inscribed on a plain slab of marble. Reverend Ashbel Green of the Second Presbyterian Church presided.

The American Philosophical Society decided to host a Eulogium in David's memory on December 17, 1796 and invitations were sent out.

President George Washington wrote that he and Martha would be in attendance. Also in response legislators, both state and federal, and bureaucrats cleared their calendars, including all of the United States Supreme Court Justices. Ordinary citizens rearranged the schedule of their chores so they too could attend. Classes were canceled by the trustees of the University and trustees of the College of Physician in order to allow professors and students alike the opportunity to attend. The members of the Philosophical Society met at their facilities a little early so they could go in a mass procession to the meeting.

All in all, the City of Philadelphia was virtually shut down. The only activity seemed to be centered around Dr. Ewing's new church, the First Presbyterian Church on High Street located between Second and Third streets. At noon the assembled crowd took their seats to hear the renown Dr. Benjamin Rush, a devoted admirer of David, give an eloquent eulogy of his departed friend. The only notable absence of attendance was David's most prized friend, Thomas Jefferson, who was at Monticello awaiting the outcome of the 1796 presidential election.

Rush knew that the eulogy had to match the articulacy of the man he praised. David had become a beloved as a myth. Rush referred to him as "the friend of God and man" who attained, with no formal education, lofty objectives that men seldom achieve. He had become the embodiment of virtues that other men could only aspire to achieve. George Washington would later offer his own assessment of David as a true founder of the country, a dedicated patriot without whose efforts the Revolution would have surely failed. David may have died, but he, and others before him, left the seed of the founder of the family, Wilhelm Rittenhouse. That seed would flourish in other famous members of the family.

In 1797 William Smith Barton, who maintained an interest in the lives of Native Americans, and the natural history of the United States, published *New Views of the Origin of the Tribes and Nations of America*, in which he corrected views he had published in a May 1787 publication, *Observations on Some Parts of Natural History*.

In his original work, he claimed he believed that the prehistoric in mounds found in Ohio were the work of Danes who made their way to America before Christopher Columbus. He corrected that by now asserting his belief that the mounds were made by Native Americans. In His original work, he stated he believed that the mounds were much older than the biblical chronology of humans established by James Ussher, and without any evidence, he also claimed that Native Americans originated in Asia. Both of those works showed that Barton was an independent thinker capable of contributing many new thoughts to the scientific literature of his day.

In 1799, a mass migration of family members began as they scattered north of Bucks County, into Canada, especially around Alberta. Others went West to Ohio, Indiana, and Michigan. Most were seeking inexpensive farmland and new frontiers that would give them more freedom from the federal government. It was a mainline belief held by most of the family members that the intrusion of government in their lives should be a minimum. Hardly any had a good word to say about Alexander Hamilton, the most visible proponent of a large strong federal government.

The Barton's were not included in those migrations. Benjamin Smith Barton had, in fact, become a physician that year in the Pennsylvania Hospital, while in 1800, Matthias was reelected to the state Senate. His younger brother, Richard Peters Barton's second son, Richard Walker Barton was born in Valley of Virginia shortly after. Margaret, David's sister, also died that year.

On June 21 of that year, David's niece, Mary, the daughter of his brother Benjamin, married Col. Michael Nourse, who later would become a hero of the war of 1812.

After his Aunt Margaret's and Uncle David's deaths, William Barton became depressed and moved back to Lancaster to spend the rest of his life in quiet solitude. It was then that he decided to write a memoir of his uncle David's life.

When Thomas Jefferson assumed the presidency in 1801, most members of the family were elated, including David's nephew, Benjamin Franklin Rittenhouse, who was Benjamin's son. He was twelve years old when his famous uncle died, and he clearly recalled conversations between his father and his uncle, as well as with the Barton's and Sergeants, about Thomas Jefferson and his friendship with the family.

However, Jefferson assumed a worsening situation with the Ottoman Empire's Barbary states of Algiers, Tripoli, Tunis. For some time prior to Jefferson's presidency the pirates in the Mediterranean had been harassing the young U.S. Navy, by raiding American ships and taking Americans hostage. They would then demand a ransom for the return.

In 1786, prior to Thomas Jefferson being elected President, he and John Adams were sent to London to negotiate with Sidi Haji Abdrahaman, Tripoli's envoy. When asked why they made war against nations that had done them no harm, Abdrahaman replied that it was written in the Koran, that all nations which had not acknowledged the Prophet were sinners, whom it was right and duty of the faithful to plunder and enslave.

Jefferson informed John Jay, The Secretary of Foreign Affairs as well as Congress about the conversation while expressing his long-held belief that paying ransom to the Muslim nations would only invite more kidnapping and the payment of more ransom.

By 1802, William's son, Benjamin Smith Barton began editing the *Philadelphia Medical and Physical Journal*". He also became vice president of the American Philosophical Society. His younger brother, William P.C. Barton, published *A Dissertation on Freedom of Navigation and Maritime Commerce, and such Rights of States Relative Thereto, as are founded on the Law of Nations.* He dedicated the paper to Thomas Jefferson, who was President of the United States at that time. Jefferson, coincidentally, was also the president of the Philosophical Society, having succeeded William's uncle David.

In 1803 Benjamin Smith Barton published *Elements of botany or Outlines of the Natural History of Vegetables*, America's first textbook botany. He also published a comparative study of linguistics, *Etymology of Certain English Words and on Their Affinity to Words in the Languages of Different European, Asiatic and American (Indian) Nations.*

On April 30, 1803, France sold 828,000 square miles to the United States, and what everyone was calling "The Louisiana Purchase". The land was mainly unexplored. It was truly a wilderness. Jefferson was anxious to find an overland passage to the Pacific, and being a naturalist, he was extremely curious about the flora and fauna of the territory. He even believed that hairy mammoths may still be lurking in the shelter of the forests.

Jefferson commissioned his personal secretary Meriwether Lewis, and Captain William Clark to explore the territory and to bring back species of flora they found. Meriwether Lewis served as the field scientist, chronicling botanical, zoological, meteorological, geographic and ethnographic information.

Before commencing on their famous trek across the country, Jefferson wanted Meriwether Lewis to consult with Dr. Benjamin Rush, Andrew Ellicott and Benjamin Smith Barton.

Dr. Rush counseled Lewis on numerous medical equipment and procedures they may need to use in the wild. Ellicott explained the basics of astronomy to Lewis, and also taught him how to use surveying equipment. Barton, who just published *Elements of Botany or Outlines of the Natural History of Vegetables,* was consulted in an effort to increase Lewis' knowledge of botany and collections skills.

Jefferson had made a point to stay in touch with David Rittenhouse's nephews, and always considered them as some of the most brilliant men America had to offer. As Jefferson's personal secretary, Lewis had met with William Barton, as well as his two sons William Barton, Jr. and Benjamin Smith Barton on many occasions. He made arrangements to meet with Rush, Ellicott, and Benjamin Smith Barton in Philadelphia before the expedition left for St. Louis.

Lewis marveled many times about the knowledge of plants, and their proper reaping, possessed by Barton.

Lewis was well aware of the publications written by Barton, and as a matter of fact, had read them all. However, actually sitting down and talking with Barton at length in his parlor, he was still amazed by the man's knowledge of botany.

Benjamin Franklin Rittenhouse idolized Thomas Jefferson due to the families long close relationship with the President. As a result, Benjamin, at the age of twenty joined the U.S. Navy as a midshipman on January 2, 1804. He will will Serve on board the USS Constellation in the first battle of Tripoli. He died nine months later of yellow fever and was buried at sea.

Shortly after Lewis and Clark had departed in 1804, Benjamin Smith Barton published a work on medical plants, "*Collections for an Essay Towards a Material Medica of the United States*" regarding the additional value of certain plants.

William Barton, Jr., who had assumed the name of Count Paul Grillon in accordance with his class's tradition of assuming the name of some celebrated man while at Princeton. He continued to use the initials P.C. when he began studying medicine that year at the University of Pennsylvania School of Medicine. He attended under the tutelage of his uncle, Benjamin Smith Barton, who had just begun his second three-year term as editor of the *Philadelphia Medical and Physical Journal.*

After nearly two-and-a-half years spent exploring the western wilderness, the Corps of Discovery, as Lewis' expedition was officially referred to, were headed home, and arrived at the frontier village of La Charrette. La Charette was a small French settlement on the Missouri River. Four days into their journey in 1804, they had camped nearby. The people were friendly, and gave them milk and eggs.

However, by the time they reached the settlement, they were out of provisions and trade goods. They had been subsisting on wild plums, and berries. Lewis, Clark, and all of their men were anxious to continue their journey home. That journey would have to wait a few days. Upon arriving at La Charrette, the people were eager to see the famous explorers, and embraced them with praise and awe. "Every person," Clark wrote in his own form of prose and spelling, "both French and Americans seem to express great pleasure at our return, and acknowledged themselves astonished in seeing us return. They informed us that we were supposed to have been lost long since."

The next day the expedition continued to St. Louis, whereupon Lewis sent a note to the postmaster asking him to delay the mail until he had the time to jot a short letter to President Jefferson telling him that they had returned. It was September 23, 1806.

In his letter to Washington, Lewis requested that Benjamin Smith Barton make drawings and catalog the 206 flora samples he retrieved during the expedition.

In 1808, Benjamin Smith Barton was elected as president of the Philadelphia Medical Society. William P.C. Barton's, *A Dissertation on Chymical Properties and Exhilarating Effects of Nitrous Oxide Gas and Its Application to Pneumatic Medicine* won him not only his medical degree from the University of Pennsylvania, but also had a giant influence on the scientific thoughts of nitrous gas, which was generally thought of as extravagant and unproven. Matthias Barton, now retired from the Senate, died, leaving behind his wife Esther Cox Barton.

A year later twenty-three-year-old William P C Barton, upon the recommendation of Doctor Benjamin Rush and Doctor Philip Physick, received a commission in the United States Navy as a surgeon. Almost immediately Barton realized that there were many reforms that the Navy had to implement, and was constantly opining about the difficulty of performing his duties.

He wasted no time in letting his superiors, including the Secretary of the Navy, know his views regarding the reforms he thought necessary. He called for the use of lemons and limes to fight scurvy long before it was accepted as a shield from the condition. Even though his outspokenness upset many of his coworkers, he persisted in his quest to correct the many problems he found. Barton went as far as to send a bottle of lime juice to the secretary of the Navy, Paul Hamilton, with the instructions to drink it in the form of lemonade.

After Congress established naval hospitals in 1811, Secretary of the Navy, Paul Hamilton, in anticipation of war with Great Britain, asked Barton to compose a set of regulations for governing the hospitals. War seemed inevitable. The relationship between the two countries had deteriorated since England passed the Orders in Council by England in 1807. The measure was an attempt to restrict America's trade with France. By 1811 England was boarding US merchant ships and forcing American shipmen to sail for England on its merchant ships. By now many in Congress, including John C. Calhoun and Henry Clay, were clamoring for war. Finally, on June 18, 1812, President James Madison asked Congress for a declaration of war against England, and a declaration of war was issued.

At that time, the two-party system in America was creating political conflict throughout the country. The Federalists, who wanted a strong central government, and closer ties to Britain, went head to head with the Democratic–Republican Party, that believed in a weak central government. The Democratic–Republican Party, in that era, was much stronger than the Federalists. The main support for the Federalists came from the North East, while the Democratic–Republicans were strong in the South and the West.

In addition, America's advancement into the Northwest Territories was being squelched by hostile Native Americans, especially those in confederation with Chief Tecumseh.

CHAPTER 11

William P.C. Barton was elated by Secretary Hamilton's request to write a manual of regulations for the United States Navy. Now he had his opportunity to cure many of the shortcomings of Navy medical care. One of his major concerns was the lack of permanent hospitals ashore.

In 1812, he started to prepare his set of regulations governing naval hospitals. Among other things, he recommended that "each hospital accommodating at least 100 men, and should maintain a staff including a surgeon, must be a college or university graduate; two surgeon's mates; a steward; a matron; and a ward master; four permanent nurses; and a variety of servants." His recommendations were submitted by Secretary Paul Hamilton to Congress. At the same time, Benjamin Smith Barton was elected as a member of the Royal Swedish Academy of Sciences.

Even though neither country was prepared for it, the second war with Great Britain was being fought up and down the eastern seacoast, and into Canada, and the Northwest territory. England was still fighting Napoleon and had few troops or warships available for war in America. President Madison believed that the state militias would sweep in to conquer Canada easily, and that the war would be over within a year. Unfortunately, that was not to be.

In America, the war was very unpopular, especially along the East Coast, making it difficult to recruit men to supplement the nation's 12,000-man army. Thus, the volunteers that the Army did recruit were under-trained, lacked discipline and performed without distinction.

Americans living on the East Coast were so against the war that in one instance, one member of Congress from Massachusetts, who also served as Chief Justice of the Court of Sessions, was mobbed on August 8, 1812, and was kicked and hit as he made his way through town.

General William Hull led the first invading American force across the Detroit River into Canada on July 12. His troops of 1,000 men were poorly trained and equipped, but they did occupy the town of Sandwich, just outside of Windsor, Ontario.

When the war broke out, the British had immediately seized control of Lake Erie under Major General Isaac Brock. They had maintained a small force of warships on the Great Lakes prior to the war. The brig, *Adams,* was the only American warship on Lake Erie, and it was not fight-ready at the onset of the war. The *Adams* became even more useless when Hull abandoned the second invasion of Canada. The *Adams* was hampered from leaving port at Detroit because the British were able to bombard the ship with its artillery stationed on the other side of the river.

A long-time sailor on the Great Lakes, Daniel Dobbins, was an escaped prisoner of the battle for Detroit. Dobbins was granted parole by taking an oath that he would not "take up arms against the United Kingdom", and was sent to Fort Malden. However, instead of sailing to the fort, he met up with General William Hull, and began supplying information to the United States regarding British ship movements on Lake Erie.

And even though several hundred Canadians joined the American forces in August, General Hull was forced to retreat across the river, only to be captured by a British force during the surrender of Detroit. Dobbins was also captured, and was in danger of being executed for disobeying the oath. However, a friend of his, British Colonel Robert Nichols, granted him safe passage to Cleveland, Ohio. From there, Dobbins made his way to Washington, and briefed Secretary of the Navy, Hamilton about the strength of the British on Lake Erie.

After Dobbins made convincing arguments that Presque Isle in Erie, Pennsylvania could be used as a naval base, Dobbins was sent there to build four gunboats. In addition, the Navy ordered two brig-rigged ships to be built as well.

With the capture of the city of Detroit, the English controlled most of Michigan, and they now had the *Adams*. They renamed the ship *Detroit*.

Several months later, American forces, again under the command of Hull, attempted to invade Canada a second time. The results were the same.

The British had been using the newly named *Detroit* and the brig, HMS *Caledonia*, to transport supplies and arms eastward along the upper reaches of the Niagara River, close to the British Fort, Erie. However, the Americans were able to capture both ships, under the direction of Lieutenant Jesse D. Elliott, and Captain Nathan Towson. Elliott was the commander of the Lake Erie operation, and the *Caledonia* was commissioned, and taken into American service.

Shortly after it was taken back by the Americans, the *Adams (Detroit)* slipped its moorings and was swept downriver. The crew was finally able to drive anchor, but the current had taken the ship within range of the British canons. After exchanging fire with the British, the crew cut its anchor cable, and the ship drifted further down river. It finally ran aground on Squaw Island where it set on fire in order to prevent from being recaptured.

Master Commandant Oliver Hazard Perry was appointed to replace Lieutenant Elliot as commander of the Lake Erie operation. After Perry made sure Presque Isle was well defended, he made his way to Lake Ontario to confer with Commodore Isaac Chauncey, the commander of the naval forces on Lake Ontario. This is where Elliott had been transferred, and was now serving under as Captain of the *USS Madison*.

Commander Robert Heriot Barclay was appointed to command the British squadron on Lake Erie. Barclay was supposed to meet the *Queen Charlotte* at Point Abino, which would have taken him to Amherstburg, a town near the mouth of the Detroit River in Essex County, Ontario, Canada, approximately 20 miles south of Detroit, Michigan.

Tardiness caused Barclay to miss that rendezvous. Consequently, he had to make the arduous trip to Amherstburg on foot. It was June 10 before he arrived. He was accompanied by only a few officers and seamen. When he took command, he had only 275 men. He determined that there were only 2,000 Pennsylvania militiamen at Perry's base at Presque Isle.

He cruised the the eastern end of Lake Erie, hoping to intercept the American vessels from Black Rock Naval shipyard. He was unsuccessful. During July and August, Barclay received two small vessels, a schooner, and a sloop.

Because Lake Ontario and the Niagara Peninsula were controlled by America, supplies for Barclay had to be carried overland from York. Barclay's squadron lacked the firepower of the Americans. It seems both Barclay and Major General Henry Procter, who commanded the British troops on the Detroit frontier, were not only expected to fight the war with the lack of manpower, but of armament as well. At one point, Procter refused an order to make an attack because he was refused reinforcements. Instead, his Indian allies persuaded him to Fort Stephenson. The attack was unsuccessful, and Procter lost a significant portion of his troops.

Around the middle of July, Perry had built the American naval power in the region to a point that its re-building was almost complete. However, the Americans were unable to leave Presque Isle due to a sandbar covered by only 5 feet of water. For two weeks, the British formed a blockade around Presque Isle on the other side of the sandbar. Both sides were at a standstill. The British could not attack because of the sandbar, and the Americans could not leave because of it.

Barclay decided to play chess with Perry. Using the weather as a facade, he lifted the blockade for about four days. He knew Perry would try to leave Presque Isle when he was gone. If he could return at the right moment, he might be able to catch the Americans in disarray. Besides, he needed to restock his supplies, and he had a banquet in his honor to attend.

Perry immediately began to move his vessels across the sandbar as Barclay had hoped. Perry didn't know how long it would be before Barclay would be back so he felt an urgency to get into the open waters as quickly as possible.

Because they were working furiously to complete the job as quickly as possible, the task became exhausting. Perry had to dismantle the guns and transport them to the other side of the sandbar. The smaller ones were no problem. The larger ones had to be raised over the sandbar. When Barclay returned four days later, it was just as he had hoped. He found Perry still trying to complete the escape. He realized that Perry's two largest ships were not yet action ready. However, Perry's gunboats and smaller brigs formed a defensive line with so much bravado that Barclay knew he was facing "checkmate." He withdrew and waited for the completion of the *HMS Detroit*. For the time being, Perry had won.

"Who's in charge here?" Perry bellowed when he saw his reinforcements arrive at his Presque Isle compound. The row of streaming men came to a halt and stood at very sloppy attention. "I guess that would be me, sir," a haggard junior officer said as he stepped forward and saluted Perry.

Good Lord! Chauncey told me he was sending reinforcements. But I have never seen such a gathering of wretched souls. You must be Lieutenant Elliot?"

"Yes sir I am," Lieutenant Jesse Elliot said, snapping to an even tighter position of attention.

"How many are you?"

"One hundred and thirty, sir! I know at least 50 of them served on the *USS Constitution*." Elliott attempted to give Perry further information, but was cut off with a wave of a hand. A disheartened Perry knew he would have to depend on the sailors sent to him by Chauncey, as well as a few volunteers from the Pennsylvania militia.

He decided to go to Sandusky, Ohio to meet with Major General William Henry Harrison and his Army of the Northwest. After making his presence known in Amherstburg a couple of times, Perry established an anchorage at Put-In-Bay, Ohio. Now, for five weeks, Barclay was effectively blockaded and unable to move supplies from Amherstburg. His sailors, Procter's troops, and the very large numbers of Indian warriors and their families there, quickly ran out of supplies. After receiving a last-minute reinforcement of two naval officers, three warrant officers and 36 sailors, Barclay had no choice but to put out deeper waters again, and seek battle with Perry.

But a few days before the battle, Perry told his Purser Samuel Hambleton, that he wanted a signal flag that would enable him to notify his fleet when to make their move against the British.

While thinking of an appropriate slogan to put on the flag, Hambleton quickly thought of one, and presented it to Perry.

"Sir, I am thinking "Don't give up the ship.""

"Don't give up the ship? Why they are the last words that Captain Lawrence spoke, as he lost the *Chesapeake,* and his life. No, no! I do not believe that this will raise the moral of the men. However, you are my most trusted officer, and therefore, I will sleep on it." He responded.

After making his decision, the women of Erie, Pennsylvania sewed the new flag with non-other than those exact words.

On the morning of 10 September, Barclay began his assault on Perry's squadron. As soon as they spotted Barclay's ships, they ventured out to meet him. It was a beautiful morning with a light wind crossing the bay and the lake. At first, the wind gave Barclay the advantage, but it soon shifted. With that shift in wind, Perry's vessels were picking up speed, allowing him to hopefully come close enough to open an attack. Perry had hoped to get the *Lawrence* and the *Niagara* into small cannon range quickly, but again the wind was not cooperating. In the light wind the two big brigs were now making little speed, and the *Lawrence* was being bombarded by the long guns mounted in the newly completed *Detroit.* Finally, after being hammered for close to half an hour, the *Lawrence* was unable to defend itself.

As the naval battle wore on, both sides began suffering heavy casualties. Eventually, the *Lawrence* itself was battered so badly that it was basically in splinters. Most of *Lawrence*'s crew were killed or wounded.

With no choice, Perry took his new flag and left what was left of the *Lawrence*. He had to make it half-mile through heavy gunfire to the *Niagara*, amidst small gunfire raking his rowboat and with cannonballs splashing in the water around him. After reaching *Niagara*, Perry took over and relieved Elliott of his post.

Suddenly, there was an eerie calm on the lake as though both sides were satisfied with the damage they have done.

Just as suddenly, there was a horrendous sound that echoed across the Great Lakes. The *Detroit* had collided with *Queen Charlotte*, and it was now or never for the *Niagara* to make her move.

The rigging of both ships suffered severe damage and almost every officer was killed or severely wounded. Barclay himself was severely wounded. He had previously lost his left arm in battle in 1809, now he lost the use of his other one as well as one of his legs and part of his left thigh. Most of the smaller British vessels were also disabled and adrift. Despite the disarray, the British believed that victory was theirs and that the Americans would retreat.

Instead, once aboard the *Niagara*, Perry brought the schooners into closer action. Then he directed to sail the *Niagara* straight at Barclay's damaged ships. The *Niagara* slashed through the British line ahead of *Detroit* and *Queen Charlotte*, and prepared to fire broadsides while *Caledonia* and the American gunboats fired from astern. The *Detroit* and *Queen Charlotte* finally managed to untangle themselves and found that they were unable to continue the fight and surrendered. The smaller British vessels quickly turned away from the battle and headed for safety, but they were overwhelmed by the American ships and surrendered.

Although Perry won the battle while commanding the *Niagara*, he received the British surrender on the deck of the recaptured *Lawrence*. He wanted the British to see the terrible price his men had paid.

The United States Navy was unsure of what to do with the three most battered ships. William P. C. Barton used his influence to make sure that the American brig *Lawrence* and the British ships *Detroit* and *Queen Charlotte* were converted into hospital ships.

After his ships were repaired, Perry took 2,500 soldiers to Amherstburg. The troops were able to capture the city with little opposition on September 27. About the same time, American troops marched into Detroit, and recaptured it without a shot being fired.

Despite protests from Tecumseh, the leader of a confederation of Indian tribes fighting with the English, the British army command had already prepared to leave those positions even before the British naval defeat. Though he told no one, Tecumseh's protests were based largely on a strong premonition of his death.

William Henry Harrison chased the British up the Thames River, and the two forces met on October 5. The battle, known as the Battle of Thames, resulted in Tecumseh, as well as his most experienced warrior, Chief Roundhead, a Wyandot Indian, being killed in the battle.

The control of Lake Erie for the rest of the war gave the Americans a decisive defensive advantage. The Americans were able to protect Ohio, Pennsylvania, and Western New York from attack.

The war was also being conducted along the Atlantic seacoast. Under the command of Captain Isaac Hull, the *USS Constitution* was maneuvered out of Chesapeake Bay and into the open waters of the Atlantic. She was headed for Halifax, Nova Scotia. 400 miles southeast of Halifax, the HMS *Guerriere* sighted a ship on the weather beam approaching them. The crew of the *Guerriere* soon realized it was a man-of-war, and the alarm was sounded. The crew of 263 prepared for action. When the *Constitution* hoisted American colors, the commander of the *Guerriere*, Captain Dacres instructed the 10 Americans that were part of his crew, that they would not have to fight their fellow countrymen, and ordered them below deck.

The two ships exchanged broadsides for half an hour before the American ship closed her starboard beam and cut the *HMS Guerrier's* mizzen mast in half. Switching to the other bow, the American ship raked *HMS Guerriere*, which included sweeping her decks with grapeshot and musketfire, and then the *Constitution's* crew attempted to board.

The two ships had been tangled, but were now clear of each other. Then *Guerriere's* fore and main masts went over the side, leaving her an unmanageable wreck. The crew managed to clear the debris, but it was evident the ship was quickly going down. It was rolling enough to put the main deck guns under water, and the American ship was within small arms range.

The captain of the *Guerriere's* and his officers agreed to strike the colors to avoid further casualties. Fifteen men had been killed; six more were dying from their wounds, and 59 more had been injured.

Guerriere was too badly damaged to take in, so as soon as the wounded had been taken off, she was set on fire. The *Constitution* then returned to Boston, virtually unscathed. Many people who witnessed the battle insisted that the English cannonballs had just bounced off the side of the *Constitution*. They nicknamed the *Constitution* "Old Iron Sides".

The *USS United States*, under the command of Captain Decatur, then stepped up on October 25 to capture the British frigate, *Macedonian*, and carry her back to port. Then, the *Constitution*, not to be outdone, sailed south, where, on December 29, off Bahia, Brazil, she engaged in a three-hour battle with the English frigate, *Java*. Again, "Old Iron Sides" came through the battle undamaged.

While the Atlantic Ocean battles were being evenly fought, the battle was carried to the Pacific, when English ships began interfering with American whaling enterprises. In January 1813, Captain David Porter sailed the American frigate, *Essex*, into the Pacific Ocean and began pursuing British ships, most of which carried letters of *marque*, allowing them to prey on American whalers. Heavy damage was inflicted on the English ships at the beginning of the campaign. However, by March 28, 1814, the *Essex* was captured, along with her tender, *Essex Junior*, off the shores of South America.

By 1813, the British military was winning the battle on the ground with more experienced and better-trained officers and enlistees. Most of the battles were being fought around the Great Lakes, with both sides suffering heavy losses. The mounting American losses prompted Dr. Robert Rittenhouse Barton to leave his home and practice in Rock Ridge County, Virginia, and enlist in the United States Navy as a surgeon on July 9, 1813. By the war's end he received both a bronze medal and a silver medal for meritorious duty.

The British then set their sights on the Chesapeake Bay near America's new federal capital. Starting in the middle of March 1813, a British flotilla under the command of Rear Admiral George Cockburn set up a blockade of the mouth of the bay, and began raiding towns along the bay from Virginia to Maryland.

Even in the face of the raids, US Secretary of War John Armstrong, believed that the Capitol would be safe from invasion. He continued to maintain that Maryland was the intended British target. However, with the American defeat at Bladensburg, Maryland, the way was open for British troops to enter, plunder, and burn the Capitol. President James Madison and his cabinet fled to Virginia, leaving First Lady Dolly Madison to salvage what she could out of the White House. Among other things, she saved the portrait of George Washington.

Before burning the White House, then known as the Executive Mansion, the British officers ate the supper that had been prepared for the President and his cabinet, in anticipation of their victorious return.

Shortly after, the city of Washington, D.C. was set ablaze, but a furious storm with hurricane-like winds and rain swept through the area like a giant water sprinkler and extinguished the fires. In addition, the Americans set the Naval Yard in Washington on fire to prevent capture of ships then in the yard. However, the unstable combustibles they used suddenly exploded, killing and injuring a large number of British troops. The next day the British withdrew from the capitol.

The British then began their slow movement to capture or destroy Fort McHenry at the entrance to Baltimore Harbor. By September 12, 1814, the

British were in a position to do so, and began pounding the fort with heavy fire from ships just offshore. Again, heavy torrential rain swept through the area as the British ships made one last attack, before calling in the Army.

The city of Baltimore was ordered to go dark during the bombardment, which lasted 25 hours. The only lights that could be seen were produced by shells exploding over the fort and illuminating the American flag flying over the fort. The battle inspired American lawyer, Francis Scott Key, to write the poem *"Defense of Fort McHenry"* which was later set to music as the *"Star-Spangled Banner."*

By the war's end in 1814, an estimated 15,000 Americans had lost their lives, with another 4,505 wounded, and America's Capitol burned to the ground. No territory was gained by either side.

Southern slaveholders lost about 4,000 slaves, who either joined British troops, and participated in the burning of Washington, D.C., or fled to Canada and Trinidad. Several members of the Rittenhouse family from Pennsylvania to Kentucky, and Virginia into Illinois, Ohio, and Michigan fought in the war, such as: Cpl. Freeman Rittenhouse, Riddle's Ohio Militia, (no reliable ancestry available as to relation); brothers Elijah Jr., Peter, and William Rittenhouse, (Elijah, Peter, William, Gerhard, Wilhelm). William and Peter served in Jacob Shorts Co., Mounted Rifleman, Illinois militia; their brother, Pvt. Elijah Rittenhouse, Jr served in Lieut. Col. Whiteside's Detachment, Illinois Militia; Brothers Obadiah and Peter Rittenhouse, both privates, (Garret, William, William, Gerhard, Wilhelm) saw duty in Lanier's Independent Battalion, Ohio militia; Pvts. William and Peter Rittenhouse, (Garret, William, William, Gerhard, Wilhelm) served with Capt. Samuel Judy's Company, Mounted Illinois Militia; and Pvt. Adam Rittenhouse, Johnson's Mounted, Kentucky Vol., just to name a few.

Benjamin Smith Barton succeeded to the Professorship of the Theory and Practice of Medicine following the death of David's good friend, Dr. Benjamin Rush, in 1813. Dr. Rush had not only befriended David, he was a close friend of the Bartons. William Barton, Sr., the son of Rev. Thomas Barton and David's sister, Esther published *Memoirs of the life of David*

Rittenhouse. When Thomas Jefferson learned he was writing the memoirs, Jefferson ordered six copies.

In a letter to Jefferson written in 1814, former President, John Adams stated that, "Mrs. Adams reads it with great delight, and reads to me what she finds interesting, and that is, indeed, the whole book. I have not time to hear it all." In the meantime, the family continued to grow.

William PC Barton decided he was not happy with his quickly drawn suggestions for reform of Navy hospitals submitted in 1812. In 1814, he expanded his ideas in *A Treatise Containing a Plan for the Internal Organization and Government of Marine Hospitals in the United States: Together with A Scheme for Amending and Systematizing the Medical Department of the United States Navy* which contained further recommendations of reform for the new Navy hospital system. He thought America's hospital system should be modeled after British medical facilities which he admired.

He also recommended that all hospital property should be marked, "U. S. Naval Hospital," to prevent the manifest pilferage of Naval property. He was the first to recommend employing female nurses in the United States. He recommended that the matrons he wrote of in 1812 should be discrete and reputable and should be "neat, cleanly, and tidy in her dress, and urbane and tender in her deportment. It would be the matrons' responsibility to supervise the nurses and other attendants as well as those working in the laundry, larder, and kitchen, but her main function was to ensure that patients were clean and well fed, and comfortable."

Barton's book was held in such demand that a second edition had to be printed. Barton was now regarded as a man of intellect far in advance of the times. On July 14, William P. C. Barton wed his second cousin, Esther Rittenhouse, the daughter of Elizabeth Rittenhouse and Jonathan Dickinson Sergeant.

CHAPTER 12

John Rhea Barton, PC's younger brother, began studying medicine at the University of Pennsylvania. In 1815 Benjamin Smith Barton died of tuberculosis in New York City whereupon his nephew William PC Barton, succeed him as professor of botany at the University of Pennsylvania.

On January 30, 1817, Lavina Rittenhouse (Peter, Garrett, William, William, Gerhard, Wilhelm) was born in Ohio. Her father, Peter, had fought in the war of 1812. Later that year William PC Barton's daughter, Julia is born on October 21, just hours before her grandfather, William Barton, Sr. died in Lancaster, PA. Shortly thereafter, in 1818, her father published *Vegetable Materia of the United States*.

Through the years since the Revolutionary war several US territories had been added to the union as states, but there was no specific designation as how they should be represented on the American flag. Finally, on July 1, 1818 Congress decided that the addition of a new state would be represented by a new star but that the 13 stripes representing the original colonies would remain constant. As a result the Stars & Stripes became the official flag of the United States.

That was also the year that Josiah Gorgas (Joseph Gorgas, Jacob Gorgas, Jan Jacob Gorgas & Sophia Rittenhouse, Nicholas, Wilhelm) was born. James B. Rittenhouse (Peter, Garrett, William, William, Gerhard, Wilhelm) was also born that year. William PC Barton published a *Compendium Florae Philadelphicae* which cataloged all the known plants growing in the Philadelphia area and his younger brother, John Rhea Barton received his medical degree from the University of Pennsylvania.

By now some Americans were feeling that it was the country's destiny to populate the western territories. That thought would permeate the American mind to the point American's would rather go to war than deny it. It was a situation that would continue to grow over the next few decades.

However, there was more land in the western part of the country than people to populate it. Europeans began flocking to America to claim their destiny. However, the voyage over to America was not always pleasant. The quarters were cramped and there were often food and water shortages. The only American laws regulating immigration in any way were naturalization laws. Congress was concerned about the health and safety of its new immigrants, and regulated their conditions of passage to the new country. If new immigrants died during the trip to America, they could not help in the county's westward spread.

The United States Passenger Act of 1819 provided there could be no more than two passengers for every five tons of cargo and imposed a hefty fine on the captain of the vessel for each passenger over the limit. For all ships sailing from America, the Act mandated that there should be 60 gallons of water, hundred pounds of salted provisions, hundred pounds of bread, and 1 gallon of vinegar for every passenger at the time of departure.

And under the Steerage Act, strict accounting measures were imposed on ship management to compile a list of all passengers by name, sex, age and occupation. Those numbers were to be reported to the Secretary of State every three months.

That year, two more of the early members of the family passed away, William Rittenhouse (William, William, Gerhard, Wilhelm) died in Fayette County, PA on July 24. His brother, Benjamin, also passed away that year in Montgomery County, Ohio.

The struggle over slavery in the country was starting to divide family members. The first three or four generations of Rittenhouses were staunch abolitionists. However, as the family members migrated to Virginia, and

West Virginia, and other where slave holding was permissible they became slaveholders themselves. Many married into families long established in the South, who all were slaveholders. They felt to prosper, they must conform to Southern practices.

Back in 1790, one of the first members of the family to move to the south was Richard Peters Barton (Esther, Mathias, Nicholas, Wilhelm) who was William Barton Sr. brother. He had married Martha Walker, the daughter of a prominent doctor in Dinwiddie County, Virginia. The couple lived with Martha's parents at "Kingston", the family plantation. Richard was soon able to acquire his own property, and moved his family to the Valley of Virginia including the slaves he had just purchased.

He had written a letter to his older brother William stating that he hoped William would be able to visit him on his new farm. But when William realized Richard Peter owned slaves, he politely declined his brother's invitation.

Slavery was now widely accepted by those Rittenhouses who had moved into the new Western territories such as Ohio, Indiana and Illinois as well as those who had moved to the southern states, however many of the family members who remained in the north continued to support the abolition of slavery.

Politically, most were also anti-Federalists who fought for a less encroaching federal government. When Alabama was admitted as a slave state in 1819, most of the northern members of the family were disappointed. Its admission as a slave state meant America was evenly divided between slave and non-slave states. That part of the family that remained in the north wanted Alabama admitted as a free state in the hope that the government would soon realize that slavery had no place in America. It would be another 45 years before their hopes were fulfilled.

The Rittenhouse family continued to grow with the marriage of John Charles Rittenhouse's (Jacob, Gerhard, Peter, Gerhard, Wilhelm) marriage to Regina Rochelle Wenner in Sugarloaf Pennsylvania, as well as the birth of John P Rittenhouse (Samuel, Isaac, William, Gerhard, Wilhelm), who will later become a member of the New Jersey General Assembly, and a judge in the Court of Appeals in Huntington County. Elizabeth Rittenhouse (Peter, Garrett, William, William, Gerhard, Wilhelm) was also born on September 11, 1820 in Preble County, Ohio.

In 1820, tensions began to rise even more between pro-slavery and anti-slavery factions within the U.S. Congress and across the country. A year earlier, a crucial point was reached when Missouri applied for admission as a slave state. Those against slavery were afraid Missouri's admission would upset the teetering balance between slave free states, which would make it more difficult to abolish slavery in its entirety. As a result, a two-part compromise was reached. The Congress would grant Missouri's petition, while Maine would be added to the roster of states as a free state. It also passed an amendment that drew an imaginary line across the former Louisiana Territory, establishing a boundary between free and slave regions.

It was hoped that the compromise would cool the rivalries that arose by Missouri's request for admission. One thing Congress did not want do was to set a precedent for governmental approval of slavery. What it did however was to achieve an opposite effect. It established the principle that Congress could make laws regarding an individual's personal property, including slaves.

A year later in 1821, Joseph S. Rittenhouse, (Lott, William, Gerhard, Wilhelm) a part of the family's extension into the West, died in Medina County, Ohio. And, while PC Barton was publishing a *Flora of North America*, John Rhea Barton began teaching medicine at the University of Pennsylvania. This was also when J. Richter Jones (Reverend Horatio Gates Jones & Debra Levering, Sarah Rubincam, Susannah Rittenhouse & Justice W. Rubincam, Peter, Gerhard, Wilhelm) graduated with honors from the University of Pennsylvania.

Meanwhile, in the North, egalitarian attitudes toward Black-Americans were gradually taking hold as evidenced by free Blacks being given the right to vote in New York. On January 9, 1822, Horatio Gates Jones Jr., J. Richter Jones' younger brother was born in Roxborough Pennsylvania.

The US was troubled by thought of European Countries establishing new colonies in Central and South America. Many of the central and South American countries were on the precipice of gaining their independence. Many felt European colonization would be the harbinger of war between the Latin American countries and European countries for control of central and South America. The United States, from the time of Washington, wished to be in total control of the North American continent. As it gained more and more territory from European countries, America became aware that South and Central America could be easily pickings for European countries.

John Quincy Adams, President James Monroe's Secretary of State, decided it was time to establish the principle that the United States would not interfere in Europe, and Europe must not interfere in the western hemisphere. The document was written by Adams and delivered by Monroe in his annual State of the Union Address in 1823.

Also in 1823, John Rhea Barton became a surgeon at the Philadelphia Hospital and the Philadelphia Almshouse working under the direction of Doctor Philip Physick who had recommended his brother, William PC Barton, for a commission in United States Navy in 1814.

One of John Rhea Barton's outstanding qualities was that he was ambidextrous and could perform an operation with either hand. He once performed a seven-hour-long operation without changing position.

The US government however, was not above, changing positions, especially toward Native Americans. During the early days of the country, only the federal government could trade with the indigenous native Americans. To do this the government established the system of government owned trading posts. It was hoped that such a system would lead to cooperative interaction with the Native Americans, thus making them more dependent upon government supplied goods, and more dependent to government control. This system was used by the government from 1795 to 1822 in the South and the Northwest territory. This scheme enabled the government to control trade with the Indians and accumulate one of the Indians most valued possession...fur skins. The system was abolished by the federal government in 1822, but it was not until March

11, 1824, that Secretary of War, John C. Calhoun created the Bureau of Indian Affairs as a division within his department. It was hoped that the Bureau of Indian Affairs would also make the spread of white America to the Pacific less susceptible to attacks from Indian attacks.

By 1823 the westward movement so enthralled Stephen Austin that he began searching for an area to colonize. With the aid and assistance of a Dutch financier, Baron de Bastrop, Austin chose a spot on the Brazos River in Texas that would serve as an American colony inside Mexico. He named the colony San Felipe de Austin. About the only sign of commerce in the area was a ferry that spanned the Brazos River that was operated by John McFarland.

While Austin was searching for a site in Texas, Richard Walker Barton, (Richard P. Barton, Esther Rittenhouse and Rev. Thomas Barton, Mathias, Nicholas, Wilhelm) was elected to the Virginia State Assembly for two years. At the same time, John Rhea Barton, the brother of William PC Barton, commenced practice at the Philadelphia Almshouse under Dr. Philip Physick.

It did not take long before John Rhea Barton was recognized as a surgeon of exceptional talent. He was ambidextrous and often use both hands while performing surgery. A year after Richard Walker Barton's election to the Virginia State Assembly, his older brother, Robert Rittenhouse Barton, MD, and Magdalena Harvey were married on November 11 in Fredericks County, Virginia.

Five months earlier, on June 11, William PC Barton was chosen as the president of the first naval board for the examination surgeon's mates for their fitness to become commissioned to the rank of surgeon. To the disappointment of many in the Rittenhouse family, Federalists John Quincy Adams, defeated populist Andrew Jackson for the presidency of the United States.

As a measure to help the westward movement, a plan was developed to link Lake Erie, and the other Great Lakes, with the Atlantic via a canal. It would be called the Erie Canal. A bill to fund the canal easily passed through Congress. However, Pres. James Monroe refused to sign the bill declaring it to be unconstitutional. He did not believe the federal government should fund something that wouldn't enhance the country as a whole. Therefore, the state of New York, realizing that the canal would be an economic boom for New York, decided to take the project over, funding it from the state coffers.

Money to construct the canal seemed plentiful, as did the raw labor which was provided mainly by immigrants. Construction of the canal began in 1817, and it was completed on October 25, 1825. From the beginning the canal was a success. People could now go around the Appellation mountains rather than over them. Goods and wares from the West, especially produce, now took a 10th of the time that it would normally take to reach the East Coast.

Suddenly the United States became a bustling country of opportunities and discoveries, such as the discovery of aluminum in New Harmony, Indiana in 1825. The Erie Canal provided inexpensive transportation to such states as Wisconsin and Minnesota, and Americans, as well as immigrants, took advantage, building new farms in new regions of the country.

Benjamin Rittenhouse, the great astronomer David's younger brother, died in Philadelphia on August 31, 1825 at the age of 83. He died content in the knowledge that he and his family members were, in some measure, responsible for the founding and development of this great country.

The next year, the Rittenhouse family's old friend, Thomas Jefferson, died at noon on July 4, at the age of 83. Hours later 90-year-old former Pres., John Adams, died in Massachusetts. It was the 50th anniversary of the signing of the Declaration of Independence. That coincidence was the source of awe by an adoring public.

1826, was also a year of awe in the medical profession. John Rhea Barton performed the first successful operation to restore motion to limbs due to stiffness of fibrosis. Miraculously, he performed the operation in just seven minutes and without giving anesthesia to the patient.

He also invented a bandage that provided support below the anterior of the lower jaw, now known as the Barton bandage, as well as obstetrical forceps to improve the safety of the baby's head during delivery. The forceps had one fixed curved blade, and a hinged anterior blade. The forceps are named in honor of their inventor.

By November 17, 1827, J Richter Jones (Debra Levering, Sarah Rubincam, Susannah Rittenhouse, William C, Gerard, Wilhelm) was admitted to the Philadelphia bar. As a result, he joined a long list of progeny descending from Wilhelm, who became attorneys, doctors, or college professors, as well as judges and state and federal legislators.

Also in that year, the state of New York became the second sate to make slavery illegal. When Vermont asserted its independence from both New York and New Hampshire, it had abolished slavery within its territory. The first slave auction was held in New York, then known as New Amsterdam in 1655. One hundred and seventy-two years later, on July 4, 1827, the last slaves in New York were given their freedom. It was a day that David, the "great astronomer", and many of his friends had hoped for, but did not live to see.

In 1827, Andrew Jackson once again sought the presidency of the United States, and William PC Barton was appointed Dean of the Jefferson Medical college. Jackson was running under the banner of the newly formed Democratic Party, which at that time was a populist party. He was successful, and is often given credit as the founder of the Democratic Party. Many members of the Rittenhouse family were elated, many were not. Jackson had made it well-known that the eastern Indian tribes should be relocated from their lands east of the Mississippi to government provided lands west of the Mississippi. Almost immediately after his inauguration, Congress passed the Jackson backed Indian Removal Act. The act called for the removal to be peacefully and voluntarily negotiated in the form of treaties. However, when the Indians resisted. Jackson was determined to remove them forcibly. It was the prelude to the infamous Trail of Tears, one of the darkest parts of early American history. Eventually, several thousand Indians, including women and children and older members of tribes died before the "removal" was completed.

1830 was also a busy year for William PC Barton, that year he wrote *Hints for Medical Officers Cruising in the West* Indies, he also became commanding officer of the Naval Hospital in Norfork, Virginia, while helping to develop the Naval Hospital in Philadelphia, which at that was located in Naval Asylum School.

Suddenly, machines began being invented in an effort to make the life of the ordinary person easier. The typewriter was invented a year earlier in 1829. It was unreliable and cumbersome and usually a handwritten document was quicker and easier to produce. But, before long it was refined into a useful apparatus. A year later the first semi-useful sewing machine was made in the United States. It would later be improved upon by Silas Howe and successfully marketed. Slowly, America was becoming an industrialized nation.

For Southhampton County, Virginia, however, an idyllic summer exploded into a nightmarish fall. On August 21, 1831, a couple hundred slaves, led by 30-year-old slave Nat Turner, began a rebellion that lasted several days, and spread over a vast area. Turner was a religious extremist, who often preached to his fellow slave. A few months prior to the rebellion, he believed he was chosen by God to lead an uprising that would end slavery in America. The result were up to 65 whites killed, and more than 55 blacks were exocuted for their participation, one being Nat Turner. Virginia, as well as other southern states, passed laws that would prohibit teaching slaves to read or white, as well as not allowing them to congregate for religious reasons, unless it was hosted by a white minister. The Underground Railroad would soon come into existance.

On the other hand of the spectrum, two Presbyterian ministers, John J. Shipherd and Philo Stewart, established the town of Oberlin, Ohio, in 1832, where the next year they opened Oberlin College. Oberlin College became a haven for black students. The dichotomous way whites felt against blacks, whether free or slave, was quickly changing attitudes in the country. Many more people in the north began being more sympathetic to the notion of abandonment of slavery. On the other hand, southern Democrats were expressing a willingness to go to drastic measures to preserve it.

By 1833, many people expressed their dissatisfaction with President Andrew Jackson's policies. They were specifically horrified by Indian Removal Act, and its consequences. The Republican – Democrat party was too weak and ineffectual to stop Jackson and his policies toward minority interests. Thus, political leaders, such as Henry Clay and Daniel Webster formed a new political party they called the Whig Party, which means "opposing tyranny". The new party advocated the Rule of Law, and protections for minority interests against the tyranny of the majority. It favored written and unchanging constitutions and advocated a strong Congress, as opposed to a strong president.

Richard Walker Barton, (Richard P. Barton, Esther Rittenhouse and Rev. Thomas Barton, Mathias, Nicholas, Wilhelm) a former National Republican, as well as a Member of the Virginia Assembly from 1823 and 1824 quickly joined the new party and ran for, and was elected to the Assembly once again in 1832. It would be a position he would hold until 1835.

In 1833, Barton, whose wife, Cindy Gibson had died earlier, married Carolina Marks on April 30. That was also the year that Abner Rittenhouse (William, William, Gerhard, Wilhelm) died in New Jersey.

While the clouds of war were darkening over Texas, America's March toward industrialization was reinforced with the contested invention of the mechanical reaper. After much litigation, The United States Patent and Trademark Office had to decide who was the rightful inventor of the machine. The two main litigants were Obed Hussey of Ohio, who patented a mechanical in 1833, and Cyrus McCormick, who patented a very similar machine in 1837. The issue before the Patent Court was who was the actual inventor of the mechanical reaper? While Hussey had patented his creation in 1833, McCormick claimed his machine was created in 1831. It was not until 1861, that a United States Patent Court Commissioner settled the matter. McCormick was finally declared the inventor of the mechanical reaper.

In 1835, the western part of the country exploded in a vicious war between Mexico and Texas, after Texas declared its independence. The ferocious war continued for a year and included the capture of the Alamo by the Mexicans in 1836. Even with the butchery that accompanied the Mexican government's victory at the Alamo, Texas prevailed and gained its independence that year. Now the question that tore at Texans was whether they wanted to remain independent or request to become a part of the United States.

1836, was also the year that J. Richter Jones (Reverend Horatio Gates Jones & Debra Levering, Sarah Rubincam, Susannah Rittenhouse & Justice W. Rubincam, Peter, Gerhard, Wilhelm) was appointed judge of the Court of Common Pleas for the County of Philadelphia.

After serving as the eighth Vice President and the tenth Secretary of State, Martin Van Buren was elected to the presidency of the United States.

By then the country's economy had been in a cycle of boom or bust, and there were high hopes for his presidency. However, within three months the financial panic of 1837 struck the country. Hundreds of banks and businesses failed. Thousands lost their lands. For about five years the United States was wracked by the worst depression thus far in its history.

Most Democrats explained the panic as the economy following its regular pattern. In truth, Jackson's financial policies were the largest contributor to the crash. He had destroyed the Second Bank of the United States, which in turn removed restrictions on the predatory practices of some state banks. In addition, there was inflated speculation in lands, based on easy bank credit, especially in the West.

Van Buren's continuation of Jackson's tactics served only to deepen and lengthen the depression. He eventually turned to a policy of governmental frugality. His austerity program was so complete that the Government even sold the tools it had used on public works.

Despite the country's financial problems Van Buren became more and more against the expansion of slavery. He even blocked the annexation of Texas because he was sure Texas would come in as a slave state. And he was right. Texas entered as a slave state in 1845.

A young gun maker received a patent for a new style pistol that would shoot multiple times before having to reload. His name was Samuel Colt, and he immediately founded a company to manufacture and sale his invention just-in-time for the panic of 1837. His business floundered for 10 years before being saved by an order from the government for 4,000 of his revolving pistols, which would be used in the Mexican War.

Despite the hard-economic times, people continued doing what people do, falling in love, getting married, and having children. Anna Josepha Nourse (Mary Rittenhouse and Col. Michael Nourse, Benjamin, Mathias, Nicholas, Wilhelm) was no exception. In 1837 she Married a young doctor by the name of Charles Augustus Hassler, just shortly after Texas officially won its independence from Mexico.

Life is sometimes filled with little ironies and sometimes with big ironies. In 1838. William PC Barton set the stage for becoming a victim of the big irony when he wrote a paper to the US secretary of the Navy in which he expressed his opposition of the creation of the position of Surgeon General of the United States Navy. Due in large part to his objections, the creation of the position was sidelined until 1842.

CHAPTER 13

After serving as a member the Virginia State Assembly from 1823 – 24 and again from 1832 – 35, Richard Walker Barton, the son of Richard Peters Rittenhouse, and the third great grandson of Wilhelm through Nicholas, is elected to the State Assembly for the 1839 session. That was also the year that Benjamin Franklin Rittenhouse, Jr., the fourth great grandson of Wilhelm through Nicholas was born.

In 1840, a change was made in the US postal system that would be the bane of letter senders from then on. The postage stamp was introduced with the first government printed postage stamp being issued on May 6, 1840.

Perhaps more dramatic was Abraham's son, Enoch Rittenhouse's, Wilhelm's third great grandson through Nicholas, decision to close the family paper mill. The mill had been in the family for 271 years, but more and more modern paper mills were being built around the country making it economically infeasible to continue operating the Rittenhouse Paper Mill. On a happier note, Julia Barton, the daughter of Esther Sargent Rittenhouse and William PC Barton married J. Dickinson Miller, MD, a third cousin who was a descendent of J. Dickinson Sgt. by his first wife.

By 1841, the first wagon trains began rolling westward to California and its promise of mild weather and fertile ground. One member of the family who did not have his eyes on California was Richard Walker Barton. He was elected to the United States Congress as a member of the Whig Party. It was an office he would hold until 1843. Perhaps more importantly,

Josiah Gorgas, the son of Joseph Gorgas, and the third great grandson of Wilhelm through Nicholas, graduated from West Point. He was sixth in a class of 52. After his graduation, he served in a variety of posts in the Artillery Corps.

In 1842, despite having advocating against the creation of the position a few years earlier William PC Barton was appointed by Pres. James Tyler as the first Chief of Medicine and Surgery for the United States Navy, thus effectively becoming the first Navy Surgeon General, though the position was not given that title until 1870. One of his closest allies was his son-in-law, J. Dickinson Miller. In keeping with his fastidiousness about his appearance, Barton suggested uniform standards for Navy physicians. Being a creature of neatness and organization, he recommended adopting a supply table so that drugs and medicals supplies could be properly purchased, dispensed and accounted for. He also recommended standardization of the administration of Navy hospitals. He was a teetotaler and firmly believed in strict control of all alcohol on board ship. To accomplish this. He implemented having boxes of whiskey identified as medical supplies. This was not a measure that set well with the enlisted men because now the distribution of alcohol required a strict accounting.

By 1843, pioneers were still looking West, but this time to Oregon rather than California. In what became known as the "The Great Migration of 1843" as many as 1000 pioneers traveled the trail to get free land in Oregon. It was a long, hard, and treacherous trip. The Pioneers suffered greatly, including death in their quest to start over again in the wide-open Oregon country. Meanwhile, back in Virginia, Richard Walker Barton lost his bid for reelection to the United States Congress.

The year 1844 brought exciting news: Samuel Morris was able to send a message by way of telegraph from Washington DC to Baltimore. Suddenly the communication age was upon us! And the family kept growing with the birth of Albert Paul Rittenhouse, Wilhelm's sixth great grandson through Gerhard, to James and Rebecca Bell Rittenhouse on May 26 in Bloomfield Ohio. He would later go on to become a member of the Missouri State Legislature in 1874-75. Fifteen years later, he would become a member of the Colorado State Legislature as well as judge of the Eighth Judicial District of Colorado.

One piece of not-so-great news for most Rittenhouses was the election of Democrat James K. Polk as president. By now most Rittenhouse's had joined the Whig Party.

In his first couple of years in office, Polk had a lot of problems to resolve. First and foremost was the annexation of Texas, which Mexico, of course, did not want to see. He also wanted to purchase California from Mexico. Mexico was not in the selling mood. Years earlier, the United States and England had agreed that territory comprising modern-day Oregon, Washington state, and British Columbia would be jointly occupied. Everyone knew at the time that it was only a temporary agreement. Polk decided that now was the time negotiate with England for a permanent solution.

Being unable to purchase California, Polk believed that if we went to war with Mexico over the annexation of Texas, he would be able to negotiate the purchase of California as part of the peace process. But he did not want to overtly start the war. He needed an excuse. That excuse came when a detachment of Mexican troops crossed the Rio Grande River and ambushed a detachment of Americans, killing some and capturing others. Gen. Zachary Taylor convinced Polk that this was the excuse he needed, and he declared war. This came with the objections of such Whig party members as congressmen Abraham Lincoln, and John Quincy Adams, as they vehemently opposed the war. They saw the war with Mexico as nothing more than a ruse to gain territory in the west that could be admitted as slave states.

Josiah Gorgas, now lieutenant is appointed chief ordinance officer under Gen. Winfield Scott in his expedition into Mexico, where on March 9, 1847, Gorgas participated in the first ever large amphibious landing operation in US history. Also in 1847, J. Richter Jones reenters private law practice when term limits prohibited him from continuing as a judge of the Court of Common Pleas for the County of Philadelphia. Sadly, Jacob Rittenhouse, Wilhelm's third great grandson through Gerhard, dies on March 8 in Sugarloaf, Pennsylvania

On February 2, 1848, Mexico and the United States enter into the treaty of Guadalupe Hidalgo, which ceded California, New Mexico,

Nevada, Utah, and most of Arizona and Colorado. The US also received parts of Texas, Oklahoma, and Wyoming. Mexico was paid $15 million with the US agreeing to pay $3.25 million of Mexico's debt to US citizens.

Now a new ripple of excitement shimmered its way across the country. Gold had been discovered in California! Thousands flocked Sutter's Mill, and other points of Northern California in search of riches and fame. Few found them. In addition, Oregon was organized as a territory which made the expansionist and the Northeast industrial complex very happy.

Lewis M Kline, the newly married husband of Emily Elizabeth Rittenhouse, daughter of Colonel Abner Rittenhouse, who had been a member of General Washington's staff during the Revolutionary War and the great- great- granddaughter of Wilhelm through Gerhard, became struck with "gold fever" shortly after their marriage on February 19, 1849.

"You know, my dearest Emily," Lewis said to his wife, as he looked up from the reaper being pulled by the only cow Lewis owned, Maybelline. He had spotted Emily bringing him lunch and water. It was the beginning of fall, 1849, but the days were still hot and sweltering. He motioned her toward a big oak tree where they could sit and shelter themselves from the hot Cumberland, Maryland sun.

"What is it Lewis?" Emily asked as the two of them sat down under the tree. Lewis was a tall, lanky man whose young face was already etched with deep lines due to harsh weather and hard work. He was 11 years older than Emily.

"You think you going to be able to pull it back up?" Emily laughed as she patted her swollen abdomen.

I can, but I don't know about you and that youngin' you're carrying. He sure is getting mighty big," Lewis said with a grin on his face.

"He's going to get a whole lot bigger before I'm relieved of him. But you are going to tell me something," she said as she handed Lewis a cup of water.

"Well, you know, we're never going to get rich plowing this old field to death. Your great- great- grandpa back in Pennsylvania didn't get rich plowing a field, neither did your great grandpa or your grandpa or your father, for that matter. My kin never faired any better either, and we ain't going to be any different."

She looked pensively at him, not really knowing what to say. "Well, but you can't start robbing banks."

"No, you know I never stoop to that," Lewis said, looking off to the west. He did not realize that she was teasing him. "But there is enough gold out there in California to make us very wealthy."

"California! Now look here, Mr. Lewis Kline," she said excitedly as she raised her head from his shoulder. "You ain't traipsing off to California looking for your fortune and leaving me here to raise the child, myself." Her shock and anger were readily apparent from the sound of her voice and the look on her face.

All Lewis could do was stare into her face while he was trying to think of an acceptable response. "I was thinking no such thing," he blurted out. "I was thinking of all three of us, you, me, and the child going, not just me. What a fine family adventure that would be!"

Emily just sat there looking at her husband with a blank look on her face. Suddenly she smiled, "it would be a fine family venture at that. I even hear that there is rich farmland out West that could be had for less than a dollar an acre. We can't go before the firstborn, though. I don't want to have a baby while in the wilderness." Lewis happily agreed. They would wait for the baby to be born before they would sell their farm and head to California.

True to his initial campaign promise, President James K Polk, a Democrat, declined to run for a second term. That opened the way for the Whig party to nominate national war hero, a reluctant Zachary Taylor in 1848. He gained the presidency as talk of secession over slavery was heard more prominently. Taylor was not a strong abolitionist, but he did believe that talk of expanding slavery further west was an exercise in futility. The

Western states simply did not have the kind of crops that would call for a plantation type economy. He also believed it was important to keep the union whole and that secession would only lead to war. It was a position that most conservative Rittenhouse's held as well.

Emily's baby was born in March 1850. It was a boy, which the couple named John Crawford Wright. Lewis made immediate arrangements to sell his farm in Cumberland, Maryland. Within a couple of months, the family would commence an overland trip to California to seek their fortune.

Taylor was only able to complete 16 months of his term before he died of cholera. Speculation swirled that he had been assassinated by poisoning. Taylor's last actions as President was the completion of the Clayton-Bulwer treaty, which concerned the neutrality of the proposed sea to sea canal, dubbed the Nicaraguan canal. Taylor died the evening of July 9, 1850. His Vice President Millard Fillmore immediately succeeded him.

Slavery, and the admission of the various states to the Union dominated Fillmore's administration. California was admitted as a free state, but its admission made it subject to a strict "Fugitive Slave Act". At the same time, Texas was flexing its muscles in an attempt to gain land from the New Mexico territory. The boundary between the two had not yet been defined, and Texas was threatening to take territory from New Mexico, by force if necessary, in a letter to Fillmore. Fillmore replied that armed aggression against New Mexico would be viewed as a foreign invasion. Shortly thereafter, a boundary dispute was congressionally defused with the establishment of the boundary between the two. Fillmore, however, did little to permanently defuse the slavery issue, due in large to Fillmore's belief that slavery could not be legislated away by the federal government.

In 1851, Josiah Gorgas was transferred to Fort Monroe in Virginia. That transfer would forever change the course of Gorgas' life. Meanwhile, in New Jersey, Hawley Olmstead Rittenhouse was born to John P. Rittenhouse and his wife Susan Hoffman. Hawley was Wilhelm's fifth great grandson through Gerhard.

In the spring of 1851, Emily became pregnant again. This time the pregnancy was a difficult one forcing Lewis to make the decision to leave the wagon train in Council Bluffs, Iowa. By September, their daughter Samantha was born. Now with two infant children, Lewis decided to remain in Iowa. The family later moved to Nebraska where he established a sorghum mill. He died of a stroke while working in the mill in September 1872. Emily would live another 31 years, dying in June 1903.

In 1852 Josiah commenced courting Amelia Gayle, the daughter of John Gayle, the former governor of Alabama.

As a young man from Pennsylvania, Josiah, had little exposure to slavery. And as a grown man, he spent most of his energy and thoughts on military matters. Now living in the South, and being engaged to the daughter of a slaveowner, he privately began a soul search about how he really felt about slavery.

There were several other catalysts that led to his questioning the morality of one man enslaving another. He had always been apolitical, but now talk of secession made him pay more attention to what the political establishment was saying. Of course, he was also influenced by his future father-in-law, who he did not want to alienate. Neither did he wish to lose his sweet Amelia.

In 1852, he had the opportunity to read the anti-slavery novel written by a northern abolitionist who had never been to the south. Harriet Beecher Stowe's "*Uncle Tom's Cabin*" had just been published. It depicted Stowe's idea of what the life on a southern plantation was like for slaves. Southerners were highly upset, and indignant. How dare a northern woman who had never been to the South, write about a subject like slavery south of the Mason-Dixon line when she had never been exposed to it.

As a result, several proslavery books deluged the market with Josiah Priest's "*The Bible Defense of Slavery*" being one of the most popular. In it, Priest tried to find justification for slavery in the Scriptures. It was a feeble attempt based on false premises and conclusions. After weighing the pros and cons of the subject, and trying to fit them into his future life he knew, regardless of how he felt about slavery, the secession of the southern states would lead to war. He also knew which side he would be fighting for. He was now an Alabamian!

One of the things that he had seen in his travels which helped him to rationalize his pro-slavery position even more, was the fact that free black men bought and sold other black people, and had done so at least since 1654. Some free blacks purchased family members as slaves, and as a protective measure for that family member. More often they purchased other black people for the same reason that white slaveholders purchased them. For profit! Gorgas even heard that a group of black slaveholders in New Orleans requested that the governor of Louisiana form black regiments who were ready to fight for the Confederacy in the event of war. How awful could slavery be if black men enslave other black men and black slaveholders are willing to fight to protect their right to do so!

While Josiah was pondering his position regarding slavery and the potential of a war of secession, halfway across the country in a little hamlet called Union City, Ohio, Mathias M. Rittenhouse, the fifth great grandson of Wilhelm through Nicholas, and his wife, Joanna C. Meely, were introducing their new son, Charles C. Rittenhouse. Charles would become the mayor of Hastings, Nebraska in 1890 and Mayor of Tropico, California in 1911.

Two years later, back in Virginia in 1854, Charles' cousin, William Crawford Gorgas, Josiah's first son, is born. He, like his father, would become a high-ranking military man. But, more importantly, he would also become a renowned man of medicine.

CPSIA information can be obtained
at www.ICGtesting.com
Printed in the USA
LVHW091424130321
681461LV00021B/225/J